GILA MONSTER

GILA MONSTER

Sandy Dengler

VICTOR BOOKS
A DIVISION OF SCRIPTURE PRESS PUBLICATIONS INC.
USA CANADA ENGLAND

Mirage Mysteries by Sandy Dengler

Cat Killer
Mouse Trapped
The Last Dinosaur
Gila Monster

Copyediting: Carole Streeter and Barbara Williams
Cover Design: Paul Higdon
Cover Illustration: John Dawson

Library of Congress Cataloging-in-Publication Data

Dengler, Sandy
Gila monster / by Sandy Dengler.
p. cm.—(Mirage mysteries ; 4)
ISBN 1-56476-238-6
1. Research institutes—Arizona—Fiction. 2. Murder—Arizona—Fiction. 3. Gila monster—Fiction. I. Title. II. Series: Dengler, Sandy. Mirage mysteries ; 4.
PS3554.E524G55 1994
813'.54—dc20 93-38158
CIP

---

1 2 3 4 5 6 7 8 9 10 Printing/Year 98 97 96 95 94

Contents

Just Deserts

Joe Rodriguez, at five-feet-eleven, weighed just over 160 pounds and almost none of it was fat. Beside him stood his partner, Tom Flaherty. Tom, six-feet-one, weighed maybe 155 if he let his unruly red hair grow really long and then soaked it. Before them crouched a thickset lizard about fourteen inches in length, weighing in at maybe two pounds.

The lizard, outweighed 157 to 1, was winning the standoff, hands down.

Hard beside the lizard lay the reason Joe and Tom stood here in the cage room of the biology department at Arizona State University. Dr. Victor Corello, director of the Venomous Animals Research Institute—VARI to the cognoscenti who worked there—lay sprawled on the cement floor turning blue.

Gary Collier, a slight, skinny, bearded man in his

early twenties, hefted a metal stick with a pincher on the end of it. "That is exactly where the Heloderma was when I came in. As I called the police it moved a couple feet; it was up against his armpit there when I came back." Collier nudged the Gila monster into its new position closer to the corpse. "About here."

Collier seemed the classic grad student found on every campus. He wore sweats and cheap running shoes. He didn't let his scraggly beard grow wild, but neither did he trim it well. He'd be bald in twenty years: his hairline was beginning to recede already. His intensity made Joe uneasy.

"So it was out loose like that?" Joe knew six different ways to kill this chunky lizard, but not how to tackle the little beast without harming it.

"That is correct. Anything more?" Collier looked at Joe, at Tom, at Ron Reynolds, the medical examiner, hovering ten feet away.

Ron glanced at Joe and shook his head.

Collier dipped the metal stick down and, by means of a trigger on its handle, grabbed the lizard around the neck with the pincher. Joe expected him to just lift up the lizard with the stick, but he didn't. He merely pinned it down. Casually, Collier leaned over, gripped the Gila monster's neck and picked it up by hand.

"Why did ye not use the stick all the way?" Tom asked.

"Might hurt him. He's pretty heavy to hang from the snakestick if you don't have to." Collier stood erect with the beaded lizard held firmly; his thumb and first finger wrapped around the creature's bulky neck, and his other three fingers, arranged on either side of one stubby foreleg, held the lizard's body. "Ever examine one up close?"

"Cannot say I have." Cautiously, slowly, Tom reached out and ran his fingers down the gorgeous black and coral beaded skin. "Much softer than I'd expect. And dry. Not slimy at all." He touched a fingertip to the lizard's stubby foot. "Wicked sharp toenails!"

"A number." Joe pointed. "Is that a number I see?"

"They're all numbered. This one's 156. So we can track the venom. You know, the venom equals that of a rattlesnake for toxicity . . . well . . . some species of rattler." Collier looked at Joe. "You want to touch it?"

Joe could have said truthfully, *I've eaten them.* But killing a Gila monster had been illegal in Arizona since the early '50s and Joe was thirty-one. No need to explain that twenty years ago his father used to take him out for a week at a time, simply living off the land, finding food and water in what most people call a desolate waste. When you're subsisting in a desert, Gila monsters are just another source of protein.

Instead he said, "I have before. Thanks." He thought a moment. "It isn't as active as you would expect. I assume that's because it's in captivity?"

Collins smiled. "They're like kids. Some are sluggish, and others are hyperactive."

Tom again ran his fingers across that glorious beaded skin. "Cold. I realize they be cold-blooded, but can they cool themselves below room temp?"

Joe frowned. He wrapped his hand around the firm, fat tail and held it. The creature was no longer chill, but its skin did not warm up beneath his touch. "Number 156 seems cooled deliberately, Mr. Collier."

Collier studied it. "Don't know why it would be, but now that you mention it, it's pretty cool in my hand here." He looked at Joe, puzzled, then at Tom. "Seen enough?" No response. He walked over to a glass terrarium perhaps three feet by eight feet and lifted the hinged plywood lid. With a gentle flick of the wrist, he dropped the Gila monster in among its two dozen or so brethren.

Tom asked, "None of the others escaped?"

"That wasn't an escape. They don't get out of there, ever. It was released. Taken out."

"Be ye certain?"

"I'm certain. Sometimes some scorpions get out—" Collier gestured toward a cabinet of covered gray drawers. "And there's crickets and cockroaches all over, but not herps. No lizards, no snakes. We make sure."

Joe looked around. "And everything in this room is poisonous?"

"Just about."

From earliest childhood Joe was a man of the outdoors. His grandfather and father both took him out into the desert, teaching him some of the ways of the past, instilling in him a love for this Arizona country of his ancestors. Joe knew rattlesnakes and Gila monsters intimately in their native habitat, as well as the plethora of harmless snakes and lizards. You automatically kept your hands and feet out of places you couldn't see. You automatically listened, not just for rattlesnake rattles but for whispered rustles in the duff. You automatically paid attention to the trail before you. Joe maintained a healthy respect, bordering on fear, for the poisonous fellow dwellers of his desert.

To Tom, Joe knew, all these poisonous creatures were academic. Curiosities. Born and raised in snakeless Ireland, he cruised through life blissfully unaware of danger at his feet.

Two freestanding banks of cages stood in the middle of the room. There must be forty cages in the block, each maybe two by two by two feet. Stacked and shoved back against the walls were other cages, terraria, and chests of drawers. Along the right-hand wall stood lab tables laden with esoteric equipment, and above them cabinets and shelves with still more stuff. Boxes and microscopes were the only things Joe could identify. The whole place, with its stark gray non-decor, gave him the willies.

Doug Hakamura came through the door. "I think we got about all of it, Joe. Ron, can you think of anything else?"

Tom cleared his throat. "Gretchen's not on this one at all, aye?"

"Nope. We've got four people out with stomach flu. She's stuck in the lab."

Ron chimed in, "But she'll be on it this afternoon. I'll have a lot of toxicology stuff for her. I want her doing the venom determination, if we have a venom here."

Joe studied Tom's gaunt profile, intrigued by the

Irishman's hesitant tone of voice.

" 'Scuse me, Joe." A uniformed officer named Frank Waller and inevitably nicknamed Fats, filled the doorway. "There's a young lady, a Ruth Houser, who says she belongs in here."

Joe looked at Gary Collier.

"She's one of Dr. Corello's doctoral students." Collier waved a hand. "Expert toxicologist, herp specialist. If anyone belongs in here, she does."

The Gila monster having been vanquished, Ron knelt on the floor to bag the body.

Joe waited until the gurney carrying the body was headed for the door. "You can let her through now, please."

Almost instantly, a startlingly attractive girl appeared in the doorway. She was built well and arranged well. She wore her long hair—a unique color somewhere between strawberry blond and medium brown—swept up and back into a gentle bun. Loose spit curls dropped down in front of her ears. She certainly knew how to clothe so shapely a body: her skirt ended a couple of inches above her knees and she had tied the tails of her rayon blouse in a knot at the front, so that her bellybutton peeped out demurely. She turned luminous green eyes first to the bag going out the door and then to Collier. He shrugged helplessly.

"Did you check the cages?" she snapped at him.

"No. Didn't think of it."

She stepped forward with nary a glance at Tom and Joe, and hurried to the banks of cages. Joe walked three steps in order to keep her in view. She peered into each cage in turn, moving rapidly down the rows—a head count, no doubt, no different from the head count that jail guards conduct periodically.

Her check completed, she glanced into each cage and terrarium along the walls. Only then did she pause to acknowledge Joe and Tom. She licked her lips. "I'm sorry. I was rude."

Joe smiled. "No apology necessary. I can say 'hello' anytime. I'd much rather know for certain that these things are all home safe. Joe Rodriguez, Tom Flaherty."

"How do you do." She smiled wanly. "Still, there's no excuse for rudeness. The campus scuttlebutt said something really hot was out loose. I was afraid it might be the boomslang. And we just got in a new *Bothrops*."

"Gila monster."

Her face went flat. "You're kidding! They . . . it can't be . . . oh, that's silly!"

Tom looked at the snake handler. "Mr. Collier. You'll be around a bit yet, aye? We'd like to talk to ye some more."

"Theoretically, I'm here till 5:00. But with your lab people locking me out so long, it'll be midnight. Sure."

"Let's pretend we're efficient," Joe suggested. "Ms. Houser. We'll need your statement as well. We . . ."

"I wasn't here. I just got here."

Joe turned on the smile again. "This isn't a 'Where were you on the morning of' session. We need facts, the more the merrier, so we glean them from everyone involved. Lots and lots of talk."

She frowned, her voice hesitant. "Doesn't sound very efficient."

"But it gets the job done."

Tom stepped forward with his native exuberance. "Meself shall mercilessly grill the youthful Ms. Houser here, whilst yourself terrorizes our Mr. Collier, aye?"

"Okay by me. By 'terrorize,' do you mean I'm not supposed to take him over to the union for a Pepsi?"

"Right. And if ye do, sit him down so that he must look upon your own phizz and cannot ogle the passing ladies."

"That's torture, all right." Joe watched Tom escort Ruth Houser out and down the hall and pondered the reactions of these two to Tommy's nonsense. Ruth plainly didn't understand it a bit and Collier let it slide right by without a smile. Both no doubt were in shock over the sudden death of their professor. Joe didn't expect guffaws, but neither did he expect the total lack of humor these two displayed. From the cartoons on the office doors in this building, and the contact he had with other people in the sciences, Gretchen in the forensics lab not the least of them, he knew that most science-oriented people enjoy a wacky, arcane, and well-developed sense of humor about the world. Gary Collier stood shuffling from foot to foot, more or less at a loss. Joe waved at random around the room. "What would you have been doing now, had we not roped off the room?"

"I'd clean snake cages, sift the poop out of the Heloderma terrarium, milk the scorpions. All the mundane little maintenance things."

"Milking scorpions is mundane?"

"Around VARI it is."

"Go ahead and do your work while we talk, if you wish."

Collins smiled, sort of. Apparently cleaning the Gila monster cage was first on the agenda. He picked up a slotted kitty-litter scoop and propped the plywood cover open.

Joe watched the lizards move about as Collier worked. None of them came remotely close to scaling the glass walls of the terrarium, though some of them curved themselves part way up, their hind feet and thick tails on the cage floor. Collier said escape was impossible; Joe would tend to agree.

Joe got out his notebook. "Tell me about Victor Corello."

"If you were a conservative white male who believes that guts, guns, and God made America great, you stood a chance of getting on his good side. I said 'a chance.' Anyone else, no chance."

"Bigoted."

"To put it mildly. No one in the world except Vic Corello knew the whole truth about absolutely everything."

"Somewhat opinionated."

Collier dropped the plywood lid back down. "We called him the Ayatollah Corello." He smirked. "Does that tell you anything?"

"What was his opinion of you?"

"Dirt." Collier picked up a snake stick shorter than the one he'd used before and headed for the freestanding bank of cages. Collier peered into a cage, opened it, and stabbed with the stick. Nonchalantly he dragged out a fat, sluggish little rattlesnake and dropped it in a tall plastic bucket. He clamped the lid on the bucket and began tidying up the cage.

He continued, "I hold tightly and fondly to certain basic precepts of the human condition. That guns are the curse of the modern race and should be banned across the board. That the ACLU serves a vital function by protecting human rights. That 90 percent of the money this government spends should be going to domestic social programs. Et cetera, et cetera."

"Diametrically opposed to all Corello believed in."

"You got it."

"Which is the majority opinion in this department, yours or his?"

Collier snorted derisively. "His. This is a redneck campus like you wouldn't believe." He stopped and frowned at Joe. "You already know that, surely. Why did you ask? Do you think. . . ?" He paused and let it go.

Which way should he take this? Joe hesitated a moment, weighing options. "Mr. Collier, if you were conducting an investigation into the death of Victor Corello, where would you start?"

"I have no idea. It's not my field."

"Speculate, please."

Collier was still frowning. "This isn't anything like the way they do it on television." His face softened; Joe could almost watch Collier's mind get caught up in the game. "I suppose . . . " His voice trailed off and he started over. "I guess I'd start with associates and family, the inner circle . . . find out who had it against him the most. Might not be where I'd end, but I guess that's where I'd start."

"So you'd be assuming an inside job. Not some stranger off the street."

Collier stared unseeing at the white plastic bucket by his feet, totally absorbed in the puzzle. "Yeah. Right. It'd have to be someone with a key to this room."

"Corello had a key. He could have let his attacker in."

"Still wouldn't be a stranger. We're pretty careful about who rates carrying a key and who gets in here. An animal activist nut decides to liberate all these poor caged critters and bingo, we have some seriously hot stuff out loose, all of it accustomed to human presence, all primed to bite somebody." He shook his head. "Has to be someone in the department."

"Are there persons in this department who would entertain enough rancor to off him?"

Collier burst out laughing. "I love the way you said that. Entertain rancor. Yeah. There isn't anyone in this department who didn't. Nearly everyone here might even say he got his just deserts." He chuckled. "I'd love being an investigator, but no thanks. There are too many suspects."

"By whom would you be employed, were you investigating?"

"By—" Collier stopped cold. "Tempe Police. Or campus cops. You said you were from Phoenix. All these people here today are Phoenix cops. Why are you guys here?" He stared at Joe as he had stared at the bucket. Joe gave him the time. He brightened into a smile of sorts. "Those Lakeside murders in the south end . . . the Tempe police are stretched too thin and the campus cops can't handle something this big. Is that it?"

Joe nodded pleasantly. "Very good, Mr. Collier. You see? You think clearly and quickly. I value highly what you have to offer because you work on a basis of fact, not speculation. Not feelings. Two and two. Four." Joe did not mention that he was using this approach to get Collier's mind, suspicious only moments ago, working on other things so that his answers would be more unguarded and spontaneous. Nor did he mention that he wanted on Collier's good side, and flattery is the smoothest, easiest means to that end.

Smugly, proudly, Collier lifted the white plastic bucket and thumped it on the floor. He popped the lid and with his stick extracted the snake. He returned it to its cage and closed the door.

"Why did you shake it up?"

"Two reasons. Disorient it so it's not waiting when I open the lid. And if it happens to be crawling up the side of the bucket, that drops it back to the bottom before I take the cover off."

"So we can pretty much assume that if something is out loose, it's deliberate. That ordinary precautions are more than adequate to prevent an accident . . . an escape."

"Have to be." Collier waved toward a big glass case against the wall. "Cascabel . . . Mexican green rattler. Its belly at the widest part is seven inches in diameter. In *diameter.* We're talking about a twenty-two-inch girth. Picture that little hummer waiting for you some morning when you open the door." He walked to another cage. "Rhinoceros viper. Over there, a boomslang; very bad news. We have three mambas. Everything you ever heard about them is true. Two genera of cobras. And we just received the *Bothrops* over in that quarantine cage. Fer-de-lance. They don't come any nastier."

"Why the zoo?"

"Research. Venom comparisons. Antivenin studies. The ones in those environmentally controlled cages, and some in the cages in the hall, are all endangered. We're doing microhabitat studies, trying to get them to breed in captivity."

"Various graduate students are conducting these studies?"

"And some of the profs who like to play with the toys." Collier leaned thoughtfully against a cage Joe wouldn't get within a yard of. "What do you automatically think when you come across a venomous snake? 'Kill it,' right? They haven't been studied. They certainly haven't been protected. And yet they hold important secrets for us. No one has ever really looked at them."

"The key to some medical breakthrough, that sort of thing?"

"If you must measure these animals by that tired old yardstick, 'Is it useful to man?' Frankly, I'm sick of it. It doesn't matter whether it's useful to man. It's a thing of beauty in its own right. It has value whether it's useful to us or not. It's part of the complete picture of life on earth. You can't kill this element of the picture and wipe out that little item without ruining the picture."

Collier stopped suddenly. He looked almost embarrassed by his ardent outburst. In silence he turned his efforts to the next cage.

"Your motivations are obvious. You're working to preserve creatures that deserve protection and appreciation and aren't getting it from the world at large. What were Corello's motivations for being here? Can you speculate?"

"Easy spec." Collier grimaced. "To enlarge the Corello name. He worked with this stuff because it's sensational. Didn't give a rip about the animals themselves. Just their headline impact. You do a paper, and then a popular book based on the paper, and a couple startling articles for popular national magazines, and your name becomes a household word. Well, more than most of us. People love to hear about this stuff, as long as they don't have to get close to it themselves. He was going to do a video. A video, for Pete's sake!"

"He was playing on morbid fascination?"

"That's it exactly. Look at Phil Osada. He just published a monograph on *Tantilla nigraceps*. Little tan snake about this long, with a black head." Collier spaced his fingers nine or ten inches apart. "Put a black-headed snake on display between a couple rattlers and nobody notices it. But that little black-headed snake is rarer and more of a curiosity than any rattler. Does Osada's name show up in the papers?" Collier blew a raspberry.

"Mr. Osada studies snakes for their own sake, in other words."

"Right. And so do I. But not Corello."

"How about Miss Houser?"

"Ruth?" Collier paused in his work. "I don't know. She's dedicated. Completely dedicated. She's done some excellent things already, and she's just getting started. She's going to be dynamite in a few years. Major, major researcher. But her deepest reasons? I couldn't tell you. I don't think Ruth knows either."

He thumped the white bucket on the floor and the rattler inside it buzzed a vicious warning.

Joe's muscles tightened and his skin tingled. He tried to imagine working in this place. Every instinct in him recoiled at the idea. He thought about the chain of events that had brought him here. His lieutenant, Jerry Hocks, avoided any milieu not paved with asphalt. Jerry was a city man to the core, and he substituted his own whims about the desert for any real understanding of it. When Tempe asked Phoenix Metro for a little interagency help, the lab especially, Jerry had instantly put Joe and Tom and Doug Hakamura's unit on it. *Snakes mean desert. Joe is a desert man. Therefore, send Joe.*

Besides, Joe was expendable. When he was partially crippled two years ago, the department lawyers became antsy. After a year of getting back, Joe was still meeting all the specs, still qualifying on all the courses. On paper he was 100 percent. But he knew and Jerry knew and the department knew his right arm and right leg were nowhere near 100 percent. He compensated.

Jerry and the lawyers wanted him to take a promotion and get off the street. Then they'd have a minority in the upper ranks, always a good thing to see in the stats, and they'd have pushed him gently out of harm's way—their harm. A promotion had its points. He wasn't high enough up the departmental ladder to receive a pension big enough to live on, let alone raise two kids. But to sit downtown and shuffle paper all day instead of getting out, matching wits, meeting people? No way, Jose.

In fact, Joe loved the fieldwork, the getting out. Except this time. Collier dumped the snake back in its cage. Its tail chirred menacingly.

This time Joe felt nothing but a deep, dismal foreboding about this whole sinuous, slithery, venomous mess.

Tea and Sympathy

Some things simply aren't made to withstand Arizona heat in July. Bring a blue spruce down from Colorado and plant it in your yard, and it will be dead in half a year, fried by heat and dryness. Display a polar bear at the Phoenix Zoo and you have to build him a climate-controlled house of his own, or he's a gone goose. Tommy Flaherty, transplanted Irishman from the coast of Galway where a heat wave is 70 degrees between lunch and supper, was not made to withstand Arizona temperatures either.

They sat in the frigid air conditioning of Tom's breakfast nook, the thermostat set on Siberia, and still Tom looked miserably overheated. Joe kept his own apartment somewhere in the low 90s, so the heat didn't knock him off his feet when he stepped outside. He could never, in all his years with Tommy, convince the Irishman that this fire and ice routine was not good for him.

Tom sipped at his quart-sized glass of iced tea and tapped a tourist pamphlet on the table. "Ruth writes these. Tourist information on local wildlife. All the tour companies and state visitor centers use her literature. She did a folder on birds, one on desert animals like coatis and peccaries, several on herps, of course."

"Herps. Reptiles and amphibians. You're picking up the lingo."

"Aye. Ye can't help it in that den of serpents."

Joe chose a folder from among the jumble of papers and supplementals scattered all over the table. "Nicely done. Rich colors. Well written." He opened the pamphlet and glanced down through some of the facts. Ruth Houser was meticulous in her accuracy. She had done an excellent job of conveying the mystery and uniqueness of Arizona's wildlife without resorting to hyperbole or sensationalism.

Joe thought a moment about what Collier had said regarding Corello and sensationalism. "Why do you think Ruth Houser is cozying up to snakes, of all things?"

Tommy propped his elbows on the table. "Methinks . . ." He spent a few more moments methinking. "Methinks she has something to prove. Ruth Houser is a lady under immense pressure. Possibly, and here I be reading betwixt the lines, working with snakes and lizards is a release from some of that pressure."

"Venomous snakes and lizards, not to mention

scorpions . . . I should think they would contribute to stress."

"Aye, for ourselves, who view such creatures with disdain, at best. But Joe, ye should see her work. She's careful; she's not about to take a chance, but she's comfortable with the creatures. They be as much an object of affection as of study."

"Prove what to whom?"

"Apparently, she's under great pressure from her momma to marry."

"What twenty-four-year-old girl isn't?"

"More so than usual, I believe. Her momma be intensely afraid she'll lose her purity and wants her safely tucked away in a marriage bed."

"Momma afraid of Corello specifically?"

"No hint. Corello was leaning heavily upon her to complete certain projects for which he would subsequently receive the lion's share of credit. She be his grad student and therefore a virtual slave in his lab."

"Sex slave? She's a beautiful woman."

Tommy pursed his lips in thought. "Aye, I'd guess, from talking to her, that he might have hit on her, possibly quite insistently. She was very circumspect on that subject. Left much to the imagination. But she's a strongly religious lady, momma or no, and keeps her nose spotless, I aver."

"So you think she resisted his advances?"

"Me first impulse is to say yes. In fact, me second impulse likewise."

"Concerned about her reputation?"

"That be another source of pressure; her papa be far more concerned about her rep than she herself, apparently. She did not say it directly, but I infer clearly that her father puts strong demands upon her behavior."

"How do you mean, exactly?"

"To assume the external trappings of the faith, ye might say." Tommy sipped heavily on his iced tea. "I surmise her father be intensely concerned about appearances. Does she attend the correct church? Does she wear the correct clothes? Does she spout the correct dogma?"

"She doesn't wear conservative clothes. In fact, she looks pretty flashy."

"Aye, flashy indeed. I detect in things she said, and her manner of dress as ye observed, that she is strenuously resisting her father's tyranny. Rebelling."

"Which in itself is pressure of a sort. Breaking away from daddy can be hard on you if your daddy's the possessive type."

"Aye! As well he appears to be. She even holds her name against him. 'Twas at her father's insistence that she be named Ruth. She feels it's dowdy and antiquated."

"So why doesn't she change it?"

"She says she's going to, but she'll wait until she marries so she can match her nice new name to her married moniker."

Joe stared at the papers all over the table. Absently he began gathering them up, dividing them into his pile and Tom's. "Any indication she's our person?"

"I saw nothing directly in her manner or in what she said. Indirectly, meself suggests she acted natural when she entered the cage room yesterday: checking the cages, concerned about an escape. And her degree of consternation—death of a power man in her life—but not a man well liked. Nothing out of line there."

"I agree. From all I could see, she's a lady in an unusual milieu, basically a man's world, functioning competently. Coping."

"Coping. Aye!" Tom nodded. "I feel a certain sympathy for her. Meself knows from me own childhood what it's like to make a life for yourself in the face of a domineering father. 'Tis a bumpy road to travel."

"And at age twenty-four she's still not completely free of his interference, apparently."

"I should think 'tis much more difficult for a daughter than for a son. Also, meself simply fled the country. Easy out. I even had the excuse. Did ye know, 75 percent of college graduates in Ireland are forced to find work outside the Auld Sod? Ruth is coping on her home turf. Her family is local. Very difficult."

Joe drained his tea. "After he finished up, Doug got a cup of coffee over at the union. He let a talkative sociology student fill him in on the campus gossip. By the time the student heard it, the story was that Corello got careless and let himself be bitten by a deadly African snake. Instant death. Then the snake chased an unidentified security man down the hall. In another version, the snake chased Ruth Houser down the hall."

The phone buzzed. Tommy twisted into a pretzel to reach the receiver on the counter behind his head. He grunted into it, listened, grunted some more, said, " 'Preciate it," and hung up.

Joe looked at him curiously.

Tommy commenced stuffing his pile of paper into his briefcase on the seat beside him. "That was Gretchen. Corello received a massive blow to the head. Whilst incapacitated, he was injected in the carotid with a hefty dose of what appears to be Gila monster venom. Ron wants her to run some tests on raw venom samples before he makes an official declaration."

"That was Gretchen, the light of your life, and you said two grunts and ' 'Preciate it'?"

"Our romance, formerly whipping along in the fast lane, has hit a speed bump."

Joe tucked his own mess of paperwork away. He'd sort it out, Xerox it, and file it later. "Little early, isn't it? It's only the middle of July. You usually break up with the girl at Christmas, so you don't have to buy a present." He scooted out of the nook and stood up.

"Rub it in, me beloved compatriot." With utter dejection pinching his lanky face, the Irishman squirmed out of his seat. "Wait!" He jogged over to his refrigerator and grabbed a stack of flyers on top of it. He handed them to Joe. "England at your fingertips. A friend of mine at a travel agency gave 'em to me for ye. She thinks ye ought to grab that offer while seats remain."

"Oh, she does." Joe leafed through the flyers. London. Stonehenge. The Yorkshire Dales. The charm of Wales. Vivid pictures in bright color beckoned. "The kids are interested, but I'm not sure.

Glo's awfully young. So is Rico, for that matter. Six and barely ten aren't exactly easy travel ages."

"They'll make it in fine fettle. Besides, Glo'll be seven by the time ye touch your tootsies onto English soil. And think of the benefit—meeting their grandparents for the first time, seeing new places, yet the language be the same. Perfect opportunity."

"You going to Ireland for sure?"

"Aye! Special price like this does not happen often." Tommy slipped into his sport coat and straightened his tie. "We best be going. Take those along. Besides the esteemed Mr. Osada, there is a John Lowry who ought to receive our attention. I made appointments with them both. Have ye seen the department secretary?"

"Long wavy hair the color of a mink coat, eyes like melted chocolate, cool and efficient as an orchestra conductor? Yes, I talked to her for an hour yesterday." He put his tea glass on the drainboard while he ran the other name through his memory. "Lowry. Lowry. Assistant professor of cytology . . . something like that."

Tom led the way out his front door. "Dr. Lowry should have gained tenure by now, but Corello has been blocking his advancement. Claims incompetence on Lowry's part."

"From your tone of voice, I assume the claim is false." Raw heat slapped Joe across his face and penetrated his lightweight sport coat instantly.

"According to Miss Watkins, the department secretary ye just described so artfully, and two others I've talked to, aye."

"Apparently Corello was hindering Osada's advancement also."

"From the sound of it, Corello hindered everything he could lay hands upon." Tommy unlocked the passenger side of his kelly green VW beetle and walked around to the driver's side.

Joe tucked and slid inside. Tom folded himself up like a carpenter's rule. Persons six-feet-one don't fit comfortably in Volkswagen bugs, but they fit even worse in MG Midgets. Besides, Joe's Midget had no air conditioning. They almost never rode in Joe's car during the heat of summer.

At the University, Joe got out at the curb and walked over to the Life Sciences building, leaving Tom to find a parking place. Joe didn't anticipate seeing him again for at least half an hour. He entered the ground floor lobby, scanned a delightful display of shorebird decoys in the display case, and looked up Osada in the directory listing by the elevator.

Third floor. Joe turned his back on the elevator and walked up the three flights.

ASU painted its Life Sciences halls the same colors hospitals use—a dead green alternated with battleship gray. Steel doors in steel moldings were the only interruptions in the stucco walls. Dismal.

Dr. Osada's door stood open. Joe rapped on the steel doorjamb and stepped inside. His office consisted of two rooms and what appeared to be a supply closet. File cabinets and a chest-high table and bar stool filled this front room. On the left wall, the door to a closet gaped open. To the right beyond another door, a desk, chairs, and file cabinets filled the second room. Joe crossed through that second door to the desk, feeling as though he should bunch his shoulders together and sidle.

A square-built, fortyish Japanese gentleman with thinning hair stood up from the desk. He looked like someone who ought to play the part of an Asian detective, or a Japanese warlord. Even though he probably didn't stand more than five-eight, he reeked of dignity and authority. "Detective Rodriguez? Right on time." He extended his hand for a shake. His grip was firm, gentle, jovial.

Joe's was not. Because of the limited use of his right hand, by habit he took a proffered hand with his right and squeezed the left over it. Ever the perfect gentleman, Osada let a flash of curiosity flit across his face but said nothing.

The whole wall to Joe's right was nothing but shelves, and on those shelves nothing but stacks of papers. At first glance this place looked chaotic. On second glance, Joe saw a clear and constant neatness to the clutter. Obviously, Dr. Osada had half enough space to work comfortably, and he made do as best he could.

"Be seated." The professor waved toward a steel-and-leather chair.

Joe sat. "I'm pleased to talk with you, despite the circumstances. Your colleagues speak glowingly of you. Black-headed snake?"

"*Tantilla nigraceps.* Yes." The man slipped smoothly from his desk to the wall of shelves. Almost without looking, he pulled a piece of paper from a stack, a second from another stack, and a half-inch-thick publication from a shelf higher than his head.

He passed them across to Joe. "Reprints of some of my work, just to give you an idea. Technical stuff; I don't expect you to wade through it, but the abstracts will tell you what's happening."

"What led you to study this obscure species, Dr. Osada?"

The man smiled gently. "Let me show you. We don't have to sit here to talk, do we?"

"No. Talk anywhere."

"Come." Dr. Osada led the way, through his jam-packed outer office, out the door, and down the hall toward the elevators. "You've been in the hot room, I assume; that is, the room with the venomous animals. Where Corello was found."

"Yes."

"Well, we're going to the cold room." He hit the down button and turned to Joe. "Black-headed snakes are as cold as you get. No venom, no animosity toward anything except insects and other such food items. They have no economic importance. They're ignored by the scientific community and unknown to the public at large." The elevator arrived and sighed its doors open.

Joe stepped inside beside him. "Did I just hear the reason you study them?"

The man's eyes twinkled. "Astute, detective! Correct!" He poked a button. The door whispered shut. "I am not a bold man. I cannot bring myself to hit the streets with protest signs, championing the homeless and the disenfranchised. So I champion the disenfranchised herps who have no voice. Literally." He paused to smile at his own pun. "I'm starting work now on *wilcoxi*, the Huachuca black-headed snake."

"Let me guess. It's found down around Wilcox."

Osada chuckled, rich and deep. "Ah, there's no stopping you, detective." He sobered. "Quite possibly, if I end up going down to San Luis Potosi, I'll gather material on both *wilcoxi* and *atriceps*. Their ranges extend about the same into Mexico."

"Kill two birds with one stone."

The elevator shuddered to a halt. Osada slapped the door sharply with the flat of his hand. He hit it again. It opened. "If you ever use this beast, that's the way to make it disgorge you." They walked the length of this hall to double doors at the end, then outside against the blast of Arizona's summer, and through more double doors into another wing of this endless quadrangular building.

They entered a room whose steel door was labeled "Authorized Personnel Only" in red. Another cage room. Like the other cage room with its deadly denizens, this one was windowless. But unlike the other, it was illuminated by soft lights in its cages. The cages in the venomous animals room had stout woven wire fronts. Each of these cages had a glass front and its own light in the hood. The combination of lighted glass fronts, some in bluish gloom and others in brightness, cast a weird illuminated-from-all-sides glow on Osada's gentle face.

Three of the four walls were lined with cages. This inside wall with the door had a table and two supply cabinets. As cluttered and disquieting as that other room was, this one exuded serenity and order.

Osada waved a hand. "None of these is a pet, yet

all of them are loved. They're specimens and test animals of students doing advanced work in physiology, ecology, and environmental studies."

Joe peered into the nearest cage. A slim, graceful whipsnake flicked its shiny black tongue at him. He looked in the next. A bulbous green blob of toad sat in a dish of water. Joe knew this momma by name, and he couldn't resist the chance to show off. "Colorado River Toad. A face only a mother could love."

Osada laughed. "*Bufo alvarius*. Yes. Here are my friends." He gestured toward cages in the corner. Joe crossed for a close look. In the upper cage he saw nothing at first. Then he picked out a small tan snake body wedged inside a cholla skeleton. The cage below it housed a more cooperative snake. It glided gracefully along between glass and sand, its black head poking here and there in the dirt.

"I've seen these." Joe stood erect. "To Indians living off the land, they're not worth catching. Too small. No food value."

Osada cocked his head. "An aspect of them I've never considered. Perhaps I can talk to you at greater length about the Indians' approach to these species and to snakes in general."

"I'd enjoy that." Joe had trouble getting his mind on business. This room fascinated him. "I assume the individualized lighting in each cage is deliberate. You're testing varying light intensities on behavior or something."

"Oversimplified, but that's it."

"Did Dr. Corello have any projects going in here?"

"No. He did not concern himself with harmless

creatures. No glory."

"So I've heard." How should Joe frame this next question? He considered a moment, and noted that Osada by nature seemed a very patient man, unhurried. "Gary Collier has been here only seven or eight months, so I didn't mention this to him, but you've been here much longer. Eighteen months ago an employee died of snakebite under very similar circumstances. Can you tell me about that?"

"Of course. It is still vivid in my memory." Dr. Osada studied cages at random, marshaling his thoughts. "His name was Jones. Jones What, I don't know. Just Jones. You know, 'Along came Jones.' He was a laborer employed by the department to do the dirty work, so to speak—clean cages, perform routine maintenance and repair. Handsome young man with little formal education beyond high school. Bright though, and upbeat. A pleasure to be around. He enjoyed the work. I found him in the hot room one afternoon. . . . "

"The same room in which Victor Corello died?"

"Yes. And a *Bothrops* out loose beside him. A fer-de-lance."

"Deadly."

"It has more notches in its gun by far than do most cobras. Security came and killed the snake, over our protest. This *Bothrops* we obtained recently is its replacement, so to speak."

"Who investigated, Tempe?"

"The head of University security then was—" Osada stopped. "I forget the word exactly. It means a genuine policeman."

"Commissioned?"

"That's it. He was empowered, so he performed the investigation."

"His finding?"

"Accidental death; carelessness when cleaning the cage."

"Did Dr. Corello have a direct hand in the investigation?"

"He assumed the position of department spokesman, liaison between the University and the press."

"I remember the hoopla."

"Hoopla, indeed."

Joe struck off on another tack. "What was Corello's opinion of your work?"

"Very low. That was a saving grace, however. I did not pose a threat, you see."

"You mean, no chance you'd hog the limelight?"

"Correct. There was one star in this production and one only. All others were supporting players. He literally blocked the projects of others he thought might garner publicity or media attention."

"All that will change now?"

"The whole department will change. And for the better." Osada pressed his lips into a thin, flat line for a moment. "I am certain you consider me a suspect. I—"

"We consider everyone a suspect."

"In this case, you're not far wrong. I can think of no one here who was not Corello's enemy at some time or other; usually all the time. I accept that I must be considered a prime suspect. He did me great harm, literally cost me years, and without professional cause."

"Rumor has it he was racist. He resisted your

advancement on racial grounds?"

"That is correct. I am a U.S. citizen, born and bred in America, as were my parents. But to him, I was ever and always 'the Jap.' I am the one he vanquished each time he watched his World War II videos."

"That sounds patently illegal. Did you ever take recourse through official channels?"

"Such maneuvers may be all right for a union in a factory. But in an academic environment, they never bear good fruit. Never. I approached him privately; I tried applying pressure within the department. Several of us did, for various reasons. He was too big, too important, too well known to dislodge."

Joe watched a delicate little gecko stalk a mealworm beetle, its cute round head cocked at a perky angle. "Was his bigotry limited to Asians?"

"By no means. All races. Even reached to certain Caucasians."

"Women?"

"Women too. With the current equal-opportunity climate, the dean insisted that he must accept a few female graduate students. No woman has ever earned a doctorate with him as her major professor."

Joe frowned and turned to him. "Ruth Houser?"

"She's still at least two years away from her degree. And now with him gone, she may have to start over. It's a serious blow to her career. Detrimental. Whoever killed him did her great harm."

"Mm." Joe looked in the next cage, a gloomy one. A long, thin snake he had never seen before hung in loops from a bare tree branch.

"You cannot imagine," Osaka continued, "how angry he would be, were he to know you are investigating his murder."

"Why me?"

Osada smiled sadly. "You're not blond."

Snake in the Grass

His feet were tired from walking on these cement floors. So were his legs. His eyes burned. His head thudded, threatening but so far not delivering on an all-out headache. His shoulders were stiff. He flexed them, trying to convince his body to hang in with it awhile longer. As much as this Life Sciences building intrigued him, Joe Rodriguez definitely was not a man of offices and laboratories. It was nearly 7:30. He wanted to go home.

Instead, he stood at a picture window looking out at a miniature desert scene. The hallway in which Joe stood ran the length of the wing, its one side a series of picture windows and its other wall blank and solid. Classroom chairs with their dinky little one-arm desks propped the doors open at both ends to let some air through, but it was hot and stuffy anyway.

Outside this second floor hall window, the four wings of the Life Sciences building enclosed an atrium not much more than fifty by eighty yards or so. The sunbaked enclosure had been converted into a natural desert of sorts, with its pink decomposed granite dirt. A palm tree, several yuccas, and a few piles of boulders formed the major elements, all picturesquely arranged. It brought to mind a one-inch-equals-one-inch scale bonsai scene.

A dozen whitewinged doves strutted around the lip of a cement water hole at this end of the compound. Pigeons lined up along the gutters of the east wing, sidling back and forth. An Abert's towhee, a little dull brown bird with a black face, poked at the weeds beside the water hole. Despite the weeds, the water hole itself was not clogged with algae or weeds, so it must be cleaned out periodically. Tarweed and incense bushes crowded around it on three sides. A sallow palo verde tree, not yet six feet high, partly shaded it.

At the other end near a jumbled pile of boulders, a young black man, clad only in jean cutoffs, raked up fallen palm fronds and duff. His well-formed muscles flexed in all the right places. Probably a jock. He looked good.

Beside Joe, Tommy stretched and yawned. "Now were it meself managing this little bit of desert, I would let the leaves and duff lie there, an integral part of the desert scene, ye see."

"I agree. But then, I wouldn't call this compound a desert."

"Eh? A dry and unwatered place of desert plants. Not exactly woodland."

"But nowhere near pristine. It represents desert, but is not itself a desert. It's artificial, a construct. So you might as well tidy it up or paint the rocks blue, or whatever you want." Apart from the doves and a few other birds, Joe saw nothing living out there.

"Eh, I see your point. Still, 'tis no good representation, if it be not cluttered with dried scratchy stuff."

"True."

The young man raked his pile of leaves and dead grass into a steep cone. He picked up a frond and tossed it on top. He stepped a foot or two up into the boulders, reaching for another dry and fallen frond.

Joe watched the kid's face contort, though he did not hear the scream. The man leaped back, stumbling, falling. A long black shadow flailed in the rocks.

Joe couldn't move. For seconds, he stood numbly, trying to process what he had just seen. Finally his muscles responded, though his mind still stared in disbelief.

"How do you get out there?" Joe saw no doors at ground level.

Tommy was already running to the hall door. He snatched up a chair. With a wide swing he tossed it against the window. The glass crashed and tinkled.

Hot dry air hit Joe in the face. He kicked out the glass shards that stuck up, perched for a moment on the sill, and, with fear and trepidation, dropped to the ground twelve feet below. As his feet hit, he rolled. Pain stabbed his left ankle.

His ankle hurt, but not enough to keep him from running. At a galloping limp he raced across the compound to the fallen young man.

Sprawled in the dirt, the kid gripped his right shoulder. "Snake!" Wild-eyed, he gestured with swinging hand toward the rocks. "D-d-d- . . . b-b-big snake!"

"We'll catch it later. How do we get out of here?" Joe grabbed the kid by the armpits and pulled him to sitting. The boy's body was slick with sweat.

"I can't . . . " The boy struggled helplessly.

"How do we get out of here?!"

"Over there. It's . . . O God, help me! The snake . . . " The kid choked on his words.

Joe let loose of the boy and wheeled. A long, thin black snake, much like a whipsnake, came gliding slackly down off the rocks. But it wasn't a whipsnake. It was different, glossier, more purposeful, deadlier looking. Joe pulled his gun. He aimed; no, he tried to aim. The front sight bobbed crazily. That hideous blackness slithered out into the open, right toward them.

Joe's gun bucked in his hands. Dust kicked up in front of the snake's nose. Joe fired again, higher, but the snake's head had already moved. The whole writhing thing, at least six feet of it, whipped aside and disappeared into the pile of leaves.

Joe jammed his gun in his belt and grabbed the kid's arms. "Up!" He hauled the boy to standing and with a mighty yank threw the kid right on over his shoulder. *The way out . . . over there,* the kid had said. That must be it over there on the south wing, a door in the brick wall.

With a twisted ankle and a heavy man on his shoulder in a fireman's carry, you'd think he wouldn't make very good time. He sprinted to the door in nothing flat. He jerked it open and dived through, from heat in waning daylight to air conditioning in a greenish fluorescent glow.

The door slammed shut.

Safe.

Joe let the slippery man down off his shoulder, eased him to the floor. Still wild-eyed, the boy worked his mouth like a drunken man. "Snake. I can't . . ." His mouth fumbled the words. He gagged. Joe rolled him to his side barely in time as the boy lost his stomach. Nausea is to be expected—Joe felt close to it himself—but this was different. The boy's black skin took on an ashen cast; his fingernails were turning blue.

A door burst open at the far end and a rent-a-cop came crashing in. "What the . . ." he blurted.

Joe pulled his badge case and waved it, his hands strangely uncoordinated. "Call 911—snakebite; and get someone down here who knows exotic snake venom."

"Rattler . . ."

"Something bigger and nastier. Don't stand there!"

The guy stared a moment, turned, and shuffled out the door.

The kid wasn't breathing. Joe rued chasing the campus cop away so quickly. He should have told him CPR was in progress. He turned the boy enough to tilt his head back, pinch off his nose and put two breaths in his mouth. The chest rose and fell obediently. Pulse? Still there, but feeble.

Something like an eternity later, a maintenance man came running in. Joe barked some orders between rescue breaths and wasn't even sure what he said. The pulse ceased. Joe launched into a full-scale CPR effort.

Tom was here, praise God! "Ye do the breathing," he said, and he positioned himself above the kid's breastbone. Joe put in two breaths and Tom assumed the cycle, thrusting down to literally squash the boy's heart empty, rising to let the heart fill again. *Five compressions and a breath. Five compressions and a breath. Keep air going into the kid's lungs; keep the blood circulating through his heart.* And all along, a hideous hidden voice kept telling Joe it would do no good.

More people crowded around now. Joe perceived Dr. Osada looming on the periphery. Good! He knew snake venom. Tommy said, "Switch!" and they switched, smoothly, Joe taking the cardiac thrusts and Tommy the breaths.

Finally, finally the paramedics arrived with their oxygen and bag mask and superior expertise. Joe literally crawled away, exhausted. He settled himself to sitting against the wall, leaning on its flat coolness, his knees up and his arms draped across them. His left ankle throbbed. He could feel it swelling tight inside his Wellington. He hoped he could get his boot off tonight. He closed his burning eyes and sucked in air and let copious sweat run down his face and chest to cool him.

Tommy plopped down to sitting beside Joe's right foot, facing him. "Hied meself to a phone to fetch help; heard shots, but did not see the exciting part. Ye get a look at the instrument of death?"

Joe nodded. "Not native. Placed there."

He watched the paramedics work on the inert black man, trying to get big round adhesive patches to stick on the sweaty skin, trying to attach him to the defibrillator that just might save his life. Joe glanced beyond Tom and pointed.

Ruth Houser stood nearby staring blankly at the paramedics. Her hands gripped her cheeks; her fingernails dug into her skin. And her lovely face twisted in raw shock.

As Joe lurched to standing, Tommy grabbed Ruth by the shoulders. He pivoted her, blocking her view of the action. Tom wrapped his lanky arms around her and encased her in a tight hug. She shuddered but she did not sob. She stared at Joe because he was in her line of sight.

"Who is he?" Joe asked.

"James Craig. Jim." She shuddered again. "Vic—Dr. Corello—used to call him Jim Crow. To his face. But he was such a sweet man. He'd do anything for you. He was so—" another of those world-shaking shudders convulsed her. "He was a friend. You know, a nice friend. A good friend. A colleague."

"A long, thin black snake, like a whipsnake only bigger, hit him out in the compound. Upper body. I couldn't put a ligature on him."

"Like a whipsnake? Black? You mean dark. But not black black." She wagged her lovely head, looking confused. "No, that's not how it looked. It was thicker . . ."

"Skinny. All black. Over six feet."

She stopped, staring. "It can't be the mamba! It . . . No." She took a deep breath and stood erect as Tommy eased his embrace. "We'd better catch it. Mambas are very good at getting into small places. And out of them. No. Gary would have reported it missing. It has to be something else. Are you sure it wasn't a. . . . Maybe it was a blacksnake or a coachwhip and Jim died of terror. It happens, you know. Jim's not used to snakes."

Tom motioned to a campus cop, a kid who couldn't be more than eighteen. "Hear me closely, lad. No one is to venture out into that compound. You've been trained about protecting a murder scene, aye? Well, 'tis a murder scene, and as such be sealed off. Understand?"

The lad nodded.

"Two exceptions to that," Joe added. "Two only. Tommy and me. We're the officers in charge."

"What can I do to help?" It was a woman's voice, soft, gentle, firm, in control. Joe wheeled.

She was what Joe's pastor called a "blue-hair lady," getting on in years but not yet elderly, plump but not fat, gray dyed blue but not old looking. She wore one of those matching pants outfits blue-hair ladies live in. Her nose came approximately to Tommy's tie tack.

Ruth made introductions. "Dorothy Stearns, this is Joe Rodriguez and Thomas Flaherty."

"How do you do. Can I help?" The woman watched Joe's face.

She offered. Joe would accept. "Yes. We need flashlights or spotlights. Heavy duty stuff. A couple snake sticks. Not the hook kind. The ones with pincers. And try to dig us out a blacklight."

"Certainly." Dorothy glided off gracefully.

Tom scowled at him, questioning. "We're catching it tonight?"

"Before it escapes from the compound and nails someone else. Besides, I don't think it's alone." Joe shrugged out of his sport coat and dragged at his tie. His shirt was soaked. He felt an intense weariness, a dread, and this business wasn't near over yet.

It took less than five minutes for Dorothy to return with the snake sticks, half a dozen four-cell flashlights, and a long-tube blacklight. More or less by default, Joe found himself heading up the party. He, Tommy, Ruth because she knew what they were doing, and Dr. Osada because he insisted, all went out into the compound hunting venomous snakes.

Joe led them directly to the leaf pile. "In there." He turned to Osada and Ruth. "The place is pretty thoroughly raked over, but still I'd like to see if I can pick up any tracks tomorrow, in good light. Besides, as Tom said, we're treating it as a murder scene. So the two of you must stay very close to Tom and me, please. Minimal impact."

"Aye," Tom added. "Normally, we insist on no impact at all; everybody out until the lab crew's done; but we don't want the lab crew falling victim to lethal serpents. 'Tis called 'securing the scene.' "

"A sack. We didn't bring a sack to put it in." Ruth turned, but Tom gripped her arm.

"We'll not be taking it alive, lass."

"It's a valuable research animal. You can't just—"

Dr. Osada purred, "Personal safety comes first,

Ruth. It's dusk now, and hard to see well."

"Yes, but . . . "

"I feel the same as you. It's frustrating. But he's right. No heroics. We kill it now, before it has a chance to escape, and we protect their lab crew." He looked at Joe. "Why do you think it isn't alone?"

"With all the excitement, its natural response should have been to retreat deeper into the rocks. But it didn't. Instead it came out toward us. I think something else is in there yet, something that would make a mamba nervous."

"Ah." Dr. Osada nodded. "Wise thinking." He frowned. "Few creatures, very few, make a mamba nervous."

"How about rattlers? Any rattlers placed out here, for example to make it seem more desert like?"

"No. Nothing like that. Some iguanas, a few chuckwallas; harmless things. Young children sometimes sneak in here. The place is quite a temptation to them. We would never put something dangerous here, for their sake if for no other reason."

Tommy picked up Jim Craig's rake and swatted off the top of the leaf cone. He batted away another layer. Another. The remaining leaves stirred. "Doctor?" He handed the rake to Dr. Osada. "Ruth, you'll shine the lights, please." He pulled his revolver.

She trained two four-cells on the leaf pile. Dr. Osada stroked away another inch of leaves. Another. Joe grasped his gun, and the pistol grip felt slippery in his sweaty hands. He was starting to shake again.

Lightning fast, a pile of coils within the leaves changed shape. Joe and Tom fired almost simultaneously. The roar echoed off the walls of the compound. The snake flopped crazily.

Calmly, Dr. Osada walked to the edge of the boulder pile and picked up a huge rock. Smoothly, he returned to the thrashing leaves and dropped the boulder on them. Quietly, he said, "I may not have pinned his head, but he won't go far."

Emboldened, Tommy flicked his pocketknife open and moved in close. He clapped the lens of his flashlight down on the snake's flailing head. With a quick stab he cut off the head. When he stood erect, he looked paler than usual.

Ruth sobbed. Tommy pulled her in close. "Hang tough, lass. You'll make it in fine shape."

For five minutes they probed the rock pile with sticks and lights. Joe decided his hunch was wrong and said so. Ruth encouraged them to look farther, for some very large snakes can hide in the smallest of places.

From the doorway, the young campus cop called to them, announcing the arrival of the department chairman himself. Joe threatened anyone who entered the compound with arrest, and that included muck-a-mucks up to and including the governor of the state. The door closed.

In the near darkness of gathering night, the blacklight picked up a gleaming glow. Scorpion. Another. Joe wondered if snake scales fluoresced in blacklight the way scorpions do. He hoped so, but you don't know. He had just about decided his surmise had to be wrong when the shadows moved.

With a snake stick, Tommy pried a rock loose and shoved it away. It tumbled to the bottom of the pile.

A sinister head poked out, tasted the air and retreated.

"What do we have?" Joe asked.

"Cobra," Dr. Osada replied. "A snake-eater. Interesting. This species does not share the same range as the mamba, yet the mamba instinctively feared it. The mamba recognized it as a snake-eater and retreated."

"Dr. Osada," Tommy asked, "please take Ruth back inside."

"I'm all right now." Her voice sounded firm.

" 'Tis no matter of being all right, lass. 'Tis the possibility of a ricochet. We may well have lead bouncing off the rocks in odd directions here. I want ye out of harm's way."

"What about you?"

"Meself gets paid for such nonsense. Go now. There's a good girl!"

Joe watched Dr. Osada accompany Ruth back to the door. The man treated her as a daughter, or a beloved niece. Protective. That was it. Osada was being very tenderly protective of her.

Joe looked at Tommy.

Tommy looked at him. "What if there be more out here besides these? Ye think of that?"

"I did. Let's look around for tracks tomorrow before Doug's crew comes in. We can check for others then."

It took them another ten minutes to worry the snake into emerging enough that Tommy could zero in with a good, solid head shot. They bent one of the sticks as they dismantled the boulder pile. Tom put another slug into the thing and they dug it out.

The cobra measured out at eight feet two inches, the mamba at two inches over seven feet when the severed head was added back on. TV crews with telephoto lenses on their minicams had a field day, shooting from the second-floor windows. A spokesman for the University appeared and made a royal fool of herself, spouting misinformation. They put a guard on the scene—uniformed Tempe officers—and called it a day.

Tom phoned the hospital. They could not resuscitate Jim Craig. The crime was murder, or at the very least negligent homicide. Who put those snakes out there? When? Why didn't someone—Gary Collier, presumably—report them missing from the cage room? Were there only two, or were there three or four?

Joe was back on the scene at dawn the next morning to examine the compound inch by inch, but rising so early was no sacrifice. Weary as he was, he was glad to get up and going. What with the ugly, wrenching dreams, he might as well have not slept at all.

Gretchen versus Chauvinist

At twenty-nine years old, Gretchen Wiemer felt like an old woman. She always felt old in midsummer, with the sun frying her at 112 degrees. Natural blonds are not made for hot, dry climates. Why did the lab crew constantly end up outside on scorchers like today, and inside during those gorgeous days the other nine months of the year? But then, in her five years with the Phoenix forensics lab, Gretchen had never had to investigate a crime scene in a rainstorm, either.

She stood in a scant bit of shade against the hot south wall, swilling a can of Diet Coke as the other three walls—all four of them, actually—radiated heat onto her. She watched Joe Rodriguez work. He stood around in the sun and it didn't seem to bother him. He wore a hat like everyone else did, but he wasn't deliberately seeking shade as the others were. He pointed off beyond a rock pile, explaining something with his gesturing hands to Doug Hakamura. Doug nodded, picked up the vacuum cleaner, and started going over the few square yards of dirt indicated.

Tommy was here too, of course. Gretchen got hot in summer, but Tommy parboiled. He turned red-faced in May and didn't cool off again until October. Why would a native Irishman pick this place of all places? Why not Seattle, with its annual Rain Festival January 1 to December 31? Why not Minnesota or New Jersey or Maine? How about Canada, a member of the big British family? She had asked him that a couple of times, and he never gave her a straight answer.

She glanced at her watch. Nine thirty. They were about done here. No more snakes, apparently, although they had uncovered a fascinating variety of lizards, plus two turtles in the pond.

Joe pointed and smiled, nodding. Tommy bobbed his head and grinned. Gretchen looked where they were looking. All she saw in the decomposed granite dirt of the open north end was a little tan ground squirrel sticking its head out of a hole. It considered the situation briefly and popped back down out of sight.

She stepped into blazing sun and crossed to Joe. "Why were you so happy to see a ground squirrel just now?"

"That means no snakes in his hole. I'm getting a little bored with snakes."

"Understatement becomes ye." Tommy drained his own soft-drink can.

"I can't think of anything else to do here, but then I never investigated a situation like this before. Any suggestions?" Gretchen spoke to Joe.

He shook his head. "I couldn't find anything unusual when I looked around this morning. No human tracks other than Craig's. One snake was released from that window over there, but I'm not sure which one. The mamba, I think. Doug might be able to confirm or deny that when he checks through his floor sweepings for scales and such. The other was released from the door we're using. Someone walked about twenty feet out into the compound and turned it loose. That someone's traces were obliterated partly by all of us walking in and out the door, and mostly by Craig raking."

"Been doing some reading about the culprits in question, Jose." Tommy spoke specifically to Joe. "Mambas be fast and aggressive, king cobras less so. Chances be excellent, therefore, that the mamba was the snake put out the window. Were it dropped or lowered down thusly, it could not swiftly reverse itself and attack its releaser. The cobra, being somewhat more sluggish, would probably just keep going when turned loose. Scant danger to its releaser. Quicksilver, the mamba, when it wants to move. So meself would vote for the mamba going out the window and the cobra out the door, on theoretical grounds."

"Sounds good. I'll vouch for the mamba's speed. It came off the rocks like water pouring. And by the time I got a second shot off, it was completely out of my sights. Lightning." Joe headed for the door in no hurry.

Gretchen fell in beside him. At five nine-and-something, she almost matched his five-eleven. Sometimes she yearned to be not just reasonably slim, which she was, but genuinely petite. She hadn't been petite since grade school. "Any hints on whether the snake was meant for Craig?" she asked Joe.

"I don't know. I've been out here all morning. No chance yet to talk to anyone. Tommy was talking to people, though, so he—" Joe stopped. "And you knew that, Gretch. All right, you two can both cut it out. I'm not going to middle-man your conversations. Gretch, you want to say something to Tommy, you say it to him. Quit this seventh-grade nonsense about not speaking, especially on the job."

"Quite a bit of nonsense we ought be quitting, ye ask me." Tom took off purposefully toward the door.

Joe started walking again and Gretchen fell in behind, feeling lower than dirt. She'd broken up with guys dozens of times. Why was this one so hard? *Because you love Tommy, Gretchen, you idiot. That's why.* "Joe? Was it two different people put the snakes out here?"

"Could be. Maybe not, from what Tommy just said. Two kinds of snakes with different behaviors might require going about it two different ways."

"But why two?"

Joe held the door for her. "Belt and suspenders? Results twice as fast? I don't know."

They stepped inside. In the far corner of the hallway, Osada, Ruth, and a medium-sized brown-haired man with thick, beetling Beau-Bridges eyebrows stood together in close conversation. The eyebrowed man wore his suit as if he had just tangled with a clothesline and these were the garments that happened to stick with him. His shirttail peeked out a bit in back.

Doug came in with his vacuum cleaner and toolbox. "Got the scales?" He stepped past Gretchen.

"And blood samples. Yep."

Doug nodded. His two assistants came through trundling the rest of the hardware. The job looked completed. Actually, Gretchen's part was just beginning. This case was giving her a bezillion tests and comparisons to run. She wearied of lab work sometimes.

A kid stuck his head in the doors at this end of the hall. "Mayday!" he yelped and disappeared.

What in blazes. . . ?

Ruth shook her head vigorously. With a grateful look on her face she disappeared out the far doors. Gretchen glanced at Joe. He looked as confused as she was. He crossed to Osada and the other man.

Tommy provided introductions. "Dr. John Lowry, Joe Rodriguez." So the man with the beetling brows was John Lowry. Cytologist. Tommy neglected to notice Gretchen, but then she wasn't supposed to be here. She should be leaving, since the forensics crew was finished

The doors at this end flew open and in sailed a man who looked vaguely like the movie actor Stephen Seagal, only without the ponytail. Or possibly Craig T. Stephens or Powers Boothe. One of those types. He acted like he owned the University.

He marched over to Osada and Lowry. "Ruth is

around here somewhere. I want to talk to her."

Osada looked blank. Innocent. "I'm sorry, Jason. You were misinformed. If I see her, what shall I tell her?"

The fellow's voice rose thirty decibels. "You can tell her she's coming home. Now. Do you realize she was on the 11 o'clock news last night? They're taking pictures of the compound and there she is with a couple other people, stretching killer snakes out on the ground."

"I didn't see the news," Osada purred, "but then I seldom watch television. A similar picture was in the paper this morning, however. Probably taken from the same window."

Joe stepped up and extended his hand. "Joe Rodriguez, Phoenix Metro Police."

The fellow named Jason stared at him a moment. "You were there too. It was you who measured the snake. You and him." He nodded toward Tom. "What's my daughter into, anyway?" He ignored the offer of a handshake.

"You're Jason Houser. I'd like to talk to you a few minutes, please. Find out what you know about the situation."

"Make an appointment." Houser pulled his wallet, yanked out a business card, and thrust it toward Joe. "I'm going to go find my daughter." He started to move but Tommy had planted himself in the way.

"And Mr. Houser, sir, what do ye plan to do when ye find her?"

"That's none of your business."

Tommy presented his badge. "I be an investigator as well, Thomas Flaherty at your service, sir, and 'tis indeed me business. Everything about this case be me concern until 'tis solved. I repeat me question."

Houser stared at him a full minute, with no way to know that no one, not anyone in the whole world, had ever won a stare-down with Tommy. His eyes flitted away. "I'm taking her home. I never approved of this advanced degree business. A proper wife and mother doesn't need a doctorate any more than a cow needs earrings. Before, it was silly. Now, it's dangerous."

"Aye, not to mention that it looks bad, being entangled in a messy business like murder. I trust, sir, yourself has never been embroiled in anything of the like."

That voice rose another twenty decibels. "I'm an honest, decent citizen, and Ruth is spotless. In every way. I have to go now." He started to push past Tom.

Gretchen slipped past Joe and touched Houser's arm. "Pardon me, Mr. Houser. Gretchen Wiemer, Phoenix forensics lab. I'd like to help you out, if I can. S'cuse me." She shouldered past Tom. "This way, sir?" She led the way on out the double doors, forcefully enough that Houser tagged along.

She turned to him in the hall. "Let me help you find her. You checked her office, of course. And you asked Miss Watkins, the secretary?"

"First thing."

"Tried to reach Ruth by phone?"

"I called her last night but she wasn't answering her phone. I went to her apartment but she wasn't there. I waited for her until past midnight. She's avoiding me. She knows I'm going to make her come home."

Gretchen's neck hairs bristled. She kept her tone light, her face relaxed. "I saw her around the place earlier today. It's such a big mess. She may not have gotten home at all last night. Several people worked through the night, and I bet she was one of them. She's one of the few who knows everything going on in the labs. Besides, I understand she's the only person here who can force the coffeemaker into turning out a decent cup of coffee. Did you try Gary's extension?"

"That Gary Collier? You're not suggesting she and he—"

"Oh, heavens no! Not that way. But with Dr. Corello checked out, the two of them have just about the whole load on their shoulders. He might know where she is."

"That's possible." His demeanor was relaxing just a bit. "I didn't try him yet, no."

"Let's go ask him. I have to pick up some toxicology materials from him anyway."

It was working. This belligerent pig was softening up a little. There are some things a woman can do easily that no man, not even Tommy with his stunning expertise as an interrogator, can hope to accomplish. Gretchen led the way to the elevators. She had absolutely no idea how to get to Gary Collier's office.

She hung back a bit. Did this Houser fellow?

Apparently. He hit the up button without looking, the scowl on his face frozen in place.

Gretchen kept it rolling. "What does Ruth normally do on Fridays, do you know? Routine, I mean."

"I don't know anything special on Fridays. I have no idea what she does here anytime that's worth anything. She doesn't even go to classes anymore. I could see, if she were still going to class, that maybe—"

"I understand she teaches several classes."

"She's too young to teach."

The elevator doors whooshed open. Gretchen stepped inside and let Houser push the buttons.

He hit 4 and turned toward her. "Are you a friend of Ruth's?"

"No. Only know her by sight. It's you I want to help. I have nothing but sympathy for a worried parent. I know how often I worried my poor mother. Didn't mean to, but that didn't help her any."

Past tense, huh? Gretchen's mom was alive and well and living in a condo in Palm Springs. This Neanderthal, though, probably wouldn't appreciate the fact that Gretchen's widowed mom, in her late fifties, taught an aerobics class and had just won the Desert Invitational Bodybuilding championship, senior division.

The elevator skidded to a halt. Nothing happened. For a swift, agonizing moment, Gretchen pictured herself stuck for three hours in this cage with a chauvinist jerk. But he swatted the elevator door a couple times with his ham-sized hand and it opened.

She let him lead. They stormed down the hall lickety-split. Houser entered an open office door uninvited. "Collier? There you are. Where's Ruth?"

Gretchen waited in the doorway.

A short, skinny young man with a beard looked up from his computer terminal. "Down in the basement with the microscope, scanning the 243 series. That is, unless this murder business has her schedule messed up." He glanced at Gretchen and stood up.

She smiled and extended her hand. "Gretchen Wiemer. I called this morning about some toxicology papers."

"Of course!" He came bounding around the end of his desk and scooped up a batch of technical reprints. "Just call me with any questions."

Gretchen thanked him and noted that either Gary Collier had been working all night or he didn't take baths as often as he ought to. She spoke a few mindless words and followed Houser back to the elevator.

Ruth Houser was not in the electron microscope room. She was not in either of the preparation labs she used.

Still toting her sheaf of reprints, Gretchen laid a hand on the chauvinist's arm. "Mr. Houser, there has to be some way to help you find her. Would you mind terribly buying me a cup of coffee? This whole day is really getting to me, and it's only a little after 10."

"Getting to me too. Sure." He had wilted from the robust and fiery man of action to a defeated and worried daddy. Again he led the way, not to the union, as Gretchen would have expected, but to a little coffee room in the basement's north wing.

A cardboard tray of doughnuts, severely picked

over, lay on the table by the coffee urn. Gretchen chose a chocolate one with colored sprinkles. Houser took a plain one without really looking at them. With her styro cup of coffee, Gretchen flopped into a chair at a little round table in the corner. Houser sat down across from her, as black as the coffee he sipped.

Gretchen kept her voice low and gentle. "It's obvious to me you don't like the idea of Ruth working here, and yet you know the place inside out. Are you a graduate from here?"

"No. No, I'm in construction. I've come around here often enough that I know the place. And my company put in the ductwork when they remodeled last year."

Gretchen smiled fetchingly. "Good honest work, construction. And you have something to show for it when you're done."

"That's true. That's very true." He sipped. He was thinking, obviously. His voice drifted. "Those psychologists talk about role models. Kids need a role model. Well, Ruth has the greatest role model in the world, her mother. Martha has never given me a moment of grief. She knows what a good wife is supposed to be, and she behaves herself. Runs the church nursery. Handles the hospitality and visitation schedule. Good church woman." His head wagged. "Not Ruth. I can't even get her to go to church some Sundays; she says she has work that can't wait."

"What do you do for the church? I mean, you yourself."

"Deacon." His voice grew firmer. "And I've been

a trustee. Building committee, of course. My line of work. I donate a lot of construction and repair and get subcontractors to work at cost. I've saved the church thousands." He even smiled slightly. "They put my name on the cornerstone of the youth hall."

"Was Victor Corello a Christian?"

Houser's head snapped around to her. He hardened. "You're an investigator too. A detective."

She raised both hands. "Not a bit. I'm a lab tech, that's all. I don't get to ask official questions. Just take samples and print out test results. Zillions of them. I was asking about Dr. Corello because he worked so closely with Ruth." She shrugged and smiled. "Besides, I just became a Christian myself a couple of months ago, and I wondered."

"You did? That's wonderful. What church?"

"Bethany Chapel on Seventh Avenue."

"Mm." He grunted noncommittally. "Vic claimed he didn't have time to go to church either, like Ruth claims, but he had a valid point. He accomplished a mountain of things. Always busy. Active in the NRA, as I am. Active politically too. Instrumental in getting some bills passed."

"Conservative politically, like you?"

"Good-thinking man." Houser nodded.

"Ever worry about him, I mean, with Ruth? They were together a lot."

"No. Certainly not. Ruth may not go to church as much as she should, but she's . . . uh . . . innocent. Vic wouldn't soil a woman's purity. Absolutely not."

The silence floated a few moments. "Besides," Houser continued, "his heart. He had heart problems, the kind where you could go any minute, you know? In fact, I'm surprised it's not his heart that killed him. Romantic activities put a strain on your heart, so I don't think he engaged in any. He was divorced."

"High blood pressure?"

"Yeah. In fact, I think he had one of those ministrokes."

"Where they keep you in the hospital a couple days in case it's a precursor to the big one?"

"Right. His health wasn't good. Too bad. It's the liberal fops who live on and on. The good die young."

Should she pursue his feelings about the victim further? No. Joe and Tom were the ones to do that. So long as she kept Houser convinced she wasn't an investigator, she'd get a lot more random stuff out of him. She'd report all this to Joe later.

She got Houser off and talking about Ruth, and about the younger brothers still at home. He encouraged the boys in college. He fought Ruth's education. He felt personally responsible for Ruth's chastity and appearance—that came through clearly—but not the boys'. If Gretchen didn't know the woman was grown, she'd think it was 1900 and Ruth was thirteen.

She pictured Houser either imagining or learning that Corello had violated his precious daughter, tainting the family honor. Would Houser kill the man? Yeah, he would, but not with a Gila monster. Gretchen could see Houser storming into the lab with a big noisy gun, not a wimpy squirt of venom from a hypodermic syringe.

She tagged along after Houser to a couple more

places Ruth might be, using him as a guide to learn the layout of the place. Then she bade him farewell. He went home dejected.

She sought out Joe. He was down in Dr. John Lowry's office, sitting alone, reading scientific reprints. She rapped on the steel doorjamb.

He glanced up. "Gretch." He paused. "Mr. Houser go home?"

"Finally." She invited herself in and plopped down on the desk at his elbow. "I'll tell you all about our conversation later. What was that 'Mayday' business?"

He laid his reprints aside. "Interesting. Corello and Houser were acquaintances."

"I got the feeling it was mutual admiration short of mutual like. Similar philosophies of life as the only bond."

Joe nodded, as though he'd not heard that before. "Whatever. Because Corello was favorably inclined toward Houser, he has free run of the place. Campus security has no legal reason to keep him out of the building. So the staff here runs interference for Ruth, keeping him out of her hair when she doesn't feel like dealing with him—which is most of the time."

"Diverting him. I see. Then that Mayday was a swift and familiar warning that Daddy was coming."

"Right. They send him piping down the wrong valleys; they even lock doors, Lowry says. If he ever starts looking for her in the women's lounge, she's lost her best hiding place."

Gretchen pondered all this a moment. "Joe, what

is it about Ruth Houser that makes these men fall all over themselves to protect her? Her father, I can see. But everyone else . . . *everyone* else in the department . . ."

"Cute. Delicate. Vulnerable looking."

"Spare me. Cute, delicate, vulnerable women are a dime a dozen."

Joe stared at his boot toes a few moments. "Trying to break free of an unreasonable man who holds higher education in very low esteem. She's long since outgrown the kind of iron control he tries to exercise. Our whole society has. I suspect they're defending Ruth's right to pursue education as much as they're defending Ruth herself. And against unreasonableness. Houser's attitudes aren't popular here, or in any academic environment. I think they're against him even more than they're for Ruth. And against his authoritarian fuming."

"So why Tommy? He's just as protective as anyone else in this snake pit."

"Tommy?"

"Open your eyes, Rodriguez."

"You're overreacting. What's going on with you and Tommy, anyway?"

"Nothing. Which is the whole issue." She stood up. "It's lunchtime. Feed me, and I'll tell you everything you ever wanted to know about Jason Houser, and more besides."

"I'm waiting for John Lowry to get out of a meeting. You can join us both for lunch and I'll hear about Houser later. Deal?"

"I never turn down a free lunch." She settled in a chair. She could read through these toxicology things while they waited.

"There is no free lunch." He returned to his reprints.

So true. Being liberated herself, she somehow ended up with the tab.

Night of the Iguana

For twenty minutes, shadows had been creeping up the rock pile by the water hole as the sun drifted downhill to the west. For all those twenty minutes, a huge, greenish, mottled lizard with comb-teeth running down its back had been perched on the pinnacle of the rock pile, its nose angled upward.

During a long, languorous moment, the shadow reached the top of the pile, casting the lizard in shade. The lizard moved forward slowly, deliberately, casually. It stepped off its perch. From boulder to boulder it picked its way down the pile. The thing had to be three feet long, nose to tail tip. Joe had never seen anything quite like it—certainly not in the Arizona wilds. It reached the ground and ambled splay-legged over to the water hole. The desert scenery, so-called, in this Life Sciences compound was hokey enough, but that exotic lizard destroyed the shaky ambience completely.

Joe heard footsteps at the end of the hall and turned away from the window.

"Detective? Those reprints we were talking about." John Lowry handed Joe a manila folder with a good quarter inch of stuff inside.

Joe wagged his head. "I have enough reading material to last me till Christmas."

Lowry offered a grimace in lieu of a smile. "Were you to end up in this business, you'd learn to read them fast. If it says, 'The P value failed to achieve significance,' that means the paper's worthless. Toss it. If they actually found something out, hit the abstract, skim the methods and materials, check out the results, and glance through the lead paragraphs of the discussion. Five minutes, max. On to the next one."

"You read huge volumes of material in your line of endeavor?"

"Endless papers. And that's just to keep up. If you want to get ahead, you wade through hundreds more. Literally. In detail."

"We on the outside hear the 'publish or perish' claim. You publish these endless papers endlessly or else what? Lose accreditation? Get passed over? Lose your job? Decline in prestige?"

"All that and more, depending on the institution. If you want to keep your head above water in VARI, you'd better be in print regularly. And that's not the popular press. 'Publish' in this context means scientific journals. Fail to produce significant work and you end up teaching at a junior college in Podunk.

Or pumping gas in Wickenburg." There was a tenseness to Lowry's voice. Joe had been noticing it all afternoon. It sounded particularly tight now, toward the close of day.

He explored a possible source for that tension. "You know someone who ended up pumping gas?"

"Yes, but not in Wickenburg. He was a promising student in many ways, a bit slow in others. Handicapped . . . MS. Got around though. Had such difficulties here that he quit in frustration."

"MS. Multiple sclerosis. Pumping gas in a wheelchair?"

"He's in a wheelchair now. Wasn't then. When he was here he was still ambulatory, although he lurched a lot."

Joe thought a moment. "How much help was Dr. Corello?"

"Corello got him kicked out."

"You just said he quit."

"That's the official line."

"I see. Who was his advisor?"

"Me. I fought for him as best I could, but I don't have the clout Corello did. I recommended he start over at another school or in some other department here. He felt because of his illness he was out of time, so to speak. He didn't have enough good years left to start over. He was right; less than a year later he was using a walker. Then the chair."

The big lizard turned away from the water hole and started back toward the rocks.

"You in contact with him yet?"

"Yes."

"I'd like his name and address."

Lowry's thick, beetling brows crushed together. "You certainly don't suspect an invalid in a wheelchair!"

"Stranger things have happened. But no, not really. I'd just like to talk to him. Did you know the Jones boy who died a year and a half ago?"

Lowry's face looked stricken; it answered the question without Lowry saying a word.

Joe asked, "Did you agree with the conclusion that it was an accidental death?"

"Certainly."

"Do you still agree, now that a nearly identical death has occurred?"

"Identical?" Lowry walked over to look out the window too. He must see that compound 100 times a day. "I wouldn't say 'identical.' Corello was an old hand at venomous animals. Jones was green, a beginner. And Gila monster venom as opposed to a fer-de-lance? That's like calling a cork gun identical to a .44 magnum."

"Both persons died of venination, with the probable culprits loose beside them."

"And both happened in the same room. I know. Corello should have died of cardiac arrest—bad heart, maybe you heard—or just plain meanness. But not the way he went." Lowry shook his head. "I'm satisfied that Jones died by accident."

"And so is everyone else?"

"Why not?"

"True." Joe turned his attention to the compound again. The lizard's tail was disappearing into a den in the rocks. Joe let the silence work on Lowry a little. Sure enough, after a few moments the cytology professor spoke.

"Jones' death upset me. As far as I'm concerned, he was inadequately trained. Corello had Ruth teach him the ropes, and she did the best she could. But she was stretched out too thin with all the other work Corello was piling on her. No time to really spend with Jones."

"You're saying it's not Ruth's fault?"

"Absolutely. In a sense, you can say Corello killed Jones; sent him into a hazardous job without adequate preparation."

"So now Gary Collier does it."

"Collier is experienced. He's spent years with reptiles. Jones had never worked with live animals before."

"How about Jim Craig, the young man who died out in this compound yesterday? Was he trained to handle venomous animals?"

Lowry chilled visibly. His voice tightened. "Not that I know of. No need to be. He didn't work with them. There should have been nothing out there that could harm him."

"Who would lay a trap for him?"

The chill deepened. Lowry turned to stare at Joe from beneath those bushy brows. "A trap. I heard that you're treating it as a murder case. I would have to call it an accident. Manslaughter, at most. Because of someone's carelessness, a snake gets out and bites someone. I can't think of anyone who would want to harm Jim Craig, let alone lay such a devious sort of trap." He shook his head. "Unthinkable. And tragic. So tragic."

"Which people would know that Craig would go

out there yesterday?"

"His supervisor. I suppose there's a list describing who does what up in the maintenance office."

"Hired by the department here or maintenance?"

"I don't know." Lowry's head wagged sadly. "Devastating. Jim's death is devastating. He held such promise. He was working his way through school. A senior this coming year, I believe."

"Good-looking young man."

"The bodybuilding?" Lowry smiled wanly. "He told me once he was into bodybuilding because it attracts the girls. I guess you'd call him something of a ladies' man. Got around. But I don't count that against him, by any means. The lady chooses. He never forced himself on any girl. He simply offered a very attractive choice."

"Do you know which girls, specifically?"

"No. Ruth might. She was his instructor in several lab classes and became something of a confidante to him. She's an easy woman to talk to. Several students confided in her comfortably."

"But they weren't an item, as such, Ruth and Craig?"

"I can't conceive of that. No. Can you imagine how high Ruth's father would blow if she dated a black man? Very attractive people, both of them, but no. I think Ruth is still too much under her father's wing. No."

"She referred to Craig as a colleague. Did Jason Houser know that Craig and she were friends?"

"I've no idea. Colleague? Yes. Craig was studying cell biology. Not exactly in Ruth's field, but close. We're all colleagues, in the broader sense."

Joe tried to sort all this and could find no puzzle pieces even remotely similar. "And in theory Craig was engaged in nonhazardous work. Raking leaves. The only animals out in the compound are totally harmless." Joe wandered to another window, to a slightly differently angled viewpoint.

"Totally. Chuckwallas. They're vegetarians. Never bite. The pond turtles are harmless. We feed them turtle food and they drag an occasional pigeon under. Should be a pair of collared lizards out there somewhere, and the usual little utas and spiny lizards you see all over. And Corello's iguanas. That's all."

Joe stopped and turned. "Say again?"

"Say what again?"

"Corello's iguanas?"

"He had an iguana project going out there. South American ctenosaurs. Big lizards with a row of spines down their backs. You've probably seen them."

"That's Corello's project!" The puzzle suddenly took on whole new proportions. "Then Corello could properly be expected to go out into the compound."

"A couple times a week or more. You think perhaps the trap, as you call it, was set for him?"

"What did he do out there?" Joe heard the elevator in the distance, and a couple of muffled thumps.

"He'd check his lizards and fill the hidden food dishes. Food with tracer elements. That's one project he didn't leave to his students. He liked his ctenosaurs. I don't know why—they aren't poisonous or rare. In fact, they're very common farther south. It seemed more a hobby to him."

Tom came roaring in through the double doors at the end of the hall. He parked beside Lowry. "Doctor, and top of the evening to ye. Ready to go, me friend?"

"Ready. Dr. Lowry, can you think of anything more?"

"No. But I'll work on the trap idea."

"Thank you. All speculations are welcome, and every little scrap of information." Joe shook hands with the man and followed Tommy toward the outside doors and the car and home. Joe was more than ready to go home.

Tommy glanced at the folder in Joe's hand. "Ah. Not near enough reading to do there. I've more for ye. The incident report on the Jones death of eighteen months ago."

"Summarize it and spare me the reading."

Tommy skipped down the winding stairs and out into the heat of the waning day. "Jones displayed all the classic symptoms of fer-de-lance venination. No one doubted 'twas what did him in. He hit his head going down. Apparently he was dead nearly three hours before Dr. Osada chanced to come upon him."

"Hit his head, huh?"

"The investigator thought nothing of it. He commented upon all the pointy table corners, cage corners and whatnot, and opined that 'twould be unusual had the lad not hit something in his fall."

"Can you tell anything from the report about the blow to the head?"

"No. Very vague. I know what you're thinking.

Think the same meself. Too much similarity. And yet, if ye have, for instance, two pedestrian traffic deaths, they're likely similar in most regards because the cause is the same. Might these two deaths be similar circumstantially only? A tough nut to crack."

"Anything at all untoward about the incident report itself?"

"Done by an amateur who thinks he be hot stuff. Other than that, no." Tommy paused at the corner, impatient as always for the WALK sign to turn from red to white.

"Toxicology supplemental?"

"Done by the medical center. Trustworthy. The man did indeed die of snakebite."

"Wound site?"

"No mention of it. Medical examiner was a name I do not recognize."

"Did they examine the snake's poison sacs?"

"Saw nothing of that sort. To what end?" The light flashed white and Tommy was instantly out in the street.

Joe jogged to catch up. "To see if the snake's venom sacs in the roof of its mouth were emptied. Did it actually bite the victim as advertised?"

Tommy stopped dead and wheeled to stare. "Begorra," he purred.

"In other words, did they answer the question, 'Did this given snake bite this given person?' It sounds like they didn't."

Tommy continued on, slower now. They reached the far shore and the sea of traffic commenced in full behind them. The WALK light didn't stay white for very long. "All manner of intriguing ramifications there. Tomorrow meself shall seek out the medical examiner who signed it and query him regarding the site of the bite, if there even be one."

There sat the kelly green bug in the front stadium lot across the next street. Home soon. Joe felt totally drained.

"Another lead," Tommy continued. "I was speaking with Ruth for an hour or so this afternoon, gathering details about the projects Corello's grad students be engaged in. She's beside herself. A blithering pile of mush inside; rock hard and stalwart on the surface. A brave lady, Joe, and sore put upon."

"Because of Corello's death?"

"Hit her wicked hard. She genuinely cared about him, 'tis obvious. And more. She lost two years' work. She may have to start over from scratch on some other project. Corello kept a tight rein on all the studies under his aegis, and didn't let the students know a mite more than they had to. She has no idea where her work should be leading her, nor how it fits in with others. They met today, closed-door session, to try to sort out the mess."

"I know. They didn't get out till nearly 1 o'clock. Lowry was in on it."

Tommy strode across the street and up over the curb, and dug down for his keys. His shoes squiched in the gravel. "Several of Corello's students, among them Gary Collier, share a little research facility out in the desert primeval. Corello was building a body of fieldwork; referred to it as a field station, but Ruth says 'tis little more than a pile of rubbish. We might find something of value there, though I've no idea what. I suggest we go check it out." He jammed his key in the door lock.

"Anyone been out there recently?"

"No idea. Possibly Collier. Ruth be not involved in it." He flopped down inside and popped the lock on Joe's side.

Joe slid into the seat. The raw heat from the vinyl upholstery burned through his clothes almost instantly. "What do you have on the slate for tomorrow?"

"Nothing. 'Tis Saturday. Were ye going to spend the day with your kids?"

"Can't. Fel left for Flag about an hour ago and took them along. I'm loose this weekend."

"Your sister took five little kids camping?" Tommy wagged his head and jumped the bug out into traffic. Tommy did not relate well to children.

"Camping and visiting Uncle Rojo. She doesn't have to go back to work till Tuesday and the kids were eager. They even promised to put up the tents and keep the dishes washed."

"In other words, desperate." Tommy turned the air conditioner up to max. "And yourself didn't go along?"

"I get them next week. Fel will take the apartment and I'll go over to the house. She'll be ready for the break." Joe watched the traffic and the heat shimmers, but his mind dwelt not on snakes but on the kids. All five, in fact, his sister Fel's three and his two.

He and Fel took turns with the kids, one week Joe and another week Fel, on odd and casual rotation depending on their various schedules. Because she was a nurse, and free-lancing, Fel's schedule fluctuated nearly as wildly as Joe's. It seemed to be working all right; the kids stayed at the house in Tempe full time, a solid home base in an uncertain world. Joe and Fel's Aunt Edna baby-sat full time. More stability. The kids needed it, what with Joe widowed and Fel divorced. And the arrangement, with the noncustodial person living in the Phoenix apartment, gave both Joe and Fel some blessed peace and privacy. Light at the end of a harried tunnel of childcare.

But what if Joe and Marie Kabrhan ended up marrying? Joe was ready to marry this minute, except that Marie was in Wisconsin 1,000 miles away. How would they handle the kids then? Joe ought to make a family again with his two. But then what about Fel? Leave her with her three? Keep the existing arrangement? None of the solutions sounded right.

He realized belatedly that as wrapped as he was in his own thoughts, Tommy was equally, and most uncharacteristically, silent as well. He glanced over at the Irishman. Tommy was a million miles away, not a safe place to be in this traffic. Joe poked him. "Either come back to earth or let me drive."

"Eh, I'll try not to scratch me paint job." He seemed to resume paying attention, so Joe let his own thoughts wander off again.

Tommy was jabbing his arm. "You're home, me doughty partner."

Joe snapped up straight. "By golly, you're right." They were parked at the curb in Joe's apartment complex. "Go out to that hut tomorrow?"

"Aye. I've a map and directions, but we ought to take your car. You're better at the exceedingly rural driving this sojourn will require."

"Five A.M.?"

"Much as I dread to say it, aye. Meself shall appear here with the warrant and breakfast goodies for on the road."

Joe nodded and crawled out. He waved as the beetle chugged off. He was so tired he wasn't tired anymore. His body worked on autopilot. He climbed the stairs to the second floor, shoved through his front door and bolted it from inside. He hit the lights and slogged zombielike to the kitchen.

On the waist-high bar between the kitchen and dining area, the answering machine blinked at him. He reached mechanically for the button to hear his messages, but the phone rang just then. He picked up the telephone receiver instead.

From Waukesha, Wisconsin came the voice of the greatest woman in the world, a woman he had met on a case in April, the first woman since Louise died who touched his heart. Joe's weariness fled. "Hello, Marie!"

"Joe?" Her voice was guarded, cautious. "How are you?"

"Fine. How are you doing?" He sat on the counter and relaxed back against the cupboards. Carefully he rested his aching ankle on the drainboard.

"I'm fine. Was that you on the network news?"

"No. No interviews, nothing big." The Corello murder. That was big; Corello was nationally known. But . . .

"Not an interview. A man just like you was measuring two big snakes that killed somebody. He looked exactly like you."

"Oh. Yeah, that was me. Looking down from an upstairs window?"

"Yes. Joe, what's going on? The announcer said the snakes attacked you. He said you shot and killed them as they were attacking you."

"That's not true. The black one hit a young man who was raking leaves and I hustled over and carried the kid out. That's all."

"You didn't shoot it?"

"Tommy did. I missed." Joe bit his tongue. Big mistake.

"So you were shooting *at* it! And it took two of you to kill it. Joe . . ."

"That announcer has it all mixed up, Marie. Look. I'm in the middle of a major investigation right now, but this weekend I'll write you a letter and explain everything. Okay?"

"Why can't you explain it now? I'm the one calling. It's my dime. I want to know now!"

"It's a long story. And it's not even all that interesting."

"Right." She paused. "Are you still able to take vacation time in August?"

"Sure. No change of plans."

"You didn't get bit, did you? By the snake?"

"No. Of course not. I told you, the kid got bit. I wasn't anywhere near. I had to jump out a second-story window to reach him."

"You *what*?"

"No big deal, Marie." *Liar liar, pants on fire!* His swollen left ankle hurt this very moment. He might even have to report it as an on-the-job injury if it didn't get better quickly, and he dreaded all the paperwork that entailed.

"Joe . . . " Her plaintive voice sounded a theme she was repeating oftener and oftener lately. "You're going to break your neck. You didn't think, did you? You just jumped. Right into a snakepit, right?"

He sighed heavily, audibly. "Every time we talk lately, it seems we end up at the same place. You're certain I'll be dead tomorrow and I can't convince you it's okay. Routine."

"Right. Deadly snakes are routine. Are you still coming to Waukesha in August?"

"Why wouldn't I?"

"I don't know. You seem upset with me or something."

"I don't like the arguing, I guess. I hate to hear us arguing."

"I hate to think about you courting death all the time. Bullets. Guns. And now, poisonous snakes."

"Look, Marie, I'm not going to be bitten by any poisonous snakes. Hear? Trust me. I'm not getting anywhere near them."

"But on the news . . . "

"Marie. Stop. Think. When I was growing up, my father and my grandfather both took me out into the desert. They taught me to live off the land, to track, to hunt. And they taught me how to stay safe around poisonous snakes. I'm taking Rico and Glo out now, when I can, to teach them what I was taught. When I say I know how to be careful around snakes, you can believe it."

"This isn't the desert, and these aren't just any old snakes. The announcer said—" Her voice paused. "I'm sorry. I can't quit worrying. Is the Ringgardner case cleared up yet?"

"Still not budged off dead center."

"Please quit saying words like 'dead center,' all right? Or 'dead on' or 'dead weight' or any of that. Have you fired your gun lately?"

"At the—" He halted his words in midstream and shifted quickly. "The . . . I guess you'd call it a target. Out on the firing range." Truth. He requalified last week. Night shoot.

"You were going to say 'at the snake' and caught yourself. I mean besides at the snake."

"No. Not besides the snake." Curse the stumble! He was too tired. He ought to be fresher, sharper, to talk to Marie, if he would allay her fears.

"And you missed it. Tommy killed it. Joe . . ."

For the next fifteen minutes they talked, and always the subject came drifting back to guns and snakes, over and over. When at last they hung up, Joe felt more tired and depressed than when he walked in.

He ought to go to her in Waukesha. Take the kids, see the sights of Wisconsin—cheese farms or something. And yet, there was that special deal on tickets to England.

Tommy thought Joe and the kids ought to go England, as he was going to Ireland. And yet, Marie . . .

Marie.

Snakes Alive!

"Ye go 2.3 miles and turn left. You'll be on a little side road, more a track than a freeway."

Joe glanced at his odometer. "That Dorothy Stearns certainly can write directions. Know anything about her?" If the road they were to turn off on was a track compared to this rut, his 'Burb's front end alignment was shot. The waddling Suburban lurched and swayed.

Tommy laid his page of directions momentarily aside. "Same as all the rest. Not a bit nonplussed that Corello be headed for his grave."

"Animosity? In Dorothy? She seems so kindhearted. She was Johnny-on-the-spot when we needed something, when Craig was hit."

"She feels strongly that Corello was engaged in experiments which were unnecessary and cruel.

Particularly a series of tests called LD50. She claims they're wrong. Know anything about such studies?"

Joe had not dug far into his mountain of reading, but he'd learned that much. "The L and D mean lethal dose, 50 means 50 percent. An LD50 is the dose that would kill 50 percent of the test animals that receive it. They seem to use white rats at VARI as the test animal of choice."

"Ye shoot doses of venom into white rats and see what kills half of them?"

"Essentially. It's all set up statistically, of course."

"Eh. No wonder this Dorothy be so upset. Torturing and butchering white rats for no reason that she can see."

"What did she say?"

"That she tried every way she could to halt Corello's studies of Gila monster venom, because nobody ever dies of Gila monster bite, ye see; she claims 'tis useless study."

"Cause him trouble?"

"As much as she could, I think."

"And he didn't get her fired?"

"She be a volunteer of sorts. The department has a program wherein ye serve as a tech, paid for by a grant fund administered from on high—Washington, mayhap—and then ye get placed in a job somewhere. She be recently widowed, and creating herself an employable skill."

"Sort of like job corps."

"Aye! Her grant has two years more to run, so she be ensconced, ye might say, awhile longer. And this will interest ye, for you're a zoo fan of the first water. She's also a docent at the zoo."

"Volunteers widely, in other words."

"Animal rights enthusiast, but not a frothing-at-the-mouth fanatic. Truly cares about animals, not causes."

"And does her part. Tried to stop Corello's venom studies, huh?"

"She has no degree, and therefore no clout at all, is the problem." Tommy sat in thought a few moments. They arrived at the 2.3 point on the odometer. A hundred feet ahead, a two-rut track went striking out to the left. Joe turned onto it and spent the next several minutes trying to prevent the Suburban's steering wheel from being wrenched out of his hands.

"A delicious irony, Jose."

"What's that?"

"Death by Gila monster poisoning. 'Twould be symbolic, ye see, because Corello was working on Gila monster venination although no one dies from it."

"Does Dorothy have a symbolic frame of mind?"

He wagged his head. "Hard to imagine, such a sweet, pleasant little gray-haired lady. Zap!"

"It's not nice to fool Mother Nature."

"Could be deadly. Meself has no plans to cross Mother Nature. Or Dorothy either, for a' that." He picked up his page of directions and read off the next entry. "Continue 4 miles until ye come to an arroyo. Cross the arroyo above the rocks and proceed another 1.3 miles. The research facility is the second of two adobe huts by a low rise on your left."

Five miles yet. They had long since left behind the last vestiges of civilization. Behind them lay the flat and featureless low desert with its knee-high scrub and occasional hip-high prickly pear. They climbed enough in elevation as they wound back through these burnt hills that a few sickly saguaros stuck up here and there. Thin, lacy creosote bushes and scattered barrel cactus stood about listlessly, not really liking their setting but too vegetational to move.

Joe guided his 'Burb across a sandy little arroyo upstream of a dozen smooth boulders in the dry streambed, following the tracks of other vehicles. He got out as soon as his wheels hit firm ground again and examined the trail ahead with care, studying tire tracks and other marks. At least three different vehicles came out here fairly often, one of them an off-road, the other two probably light pick-up trucks. Only one set of tire tracks was close enough to unique that he would know it again if he saw it. He got back in and they proceeded as the directions indicated.

Nothing more than one-room adobe shacks, two weathered buildings sat baking complacently in the fiery sun. The nearest trees grew in a wash 300 yards to the south. Who would put buildings here, when the comfort level would be so much higher over there? Joe pulled up to the second shack and parked off to the edge of a broad, bare turnaround. Tommy waited in the van while Joe worked a couple of circles, looking at tracks and traces. All the vehicles identifiable in the wash were accounted for here. Nothing unusual, nothing unexpected.

As Joe jiggled the key in the door lock until it

worked, Tommy got out and left his ten-gallon J.R. Ewing hat on the car seat. "I see the height of the door frame. Ceiling'll not be much higher. I've no intention of scuffing me best hat in a room built by midgets." He fired up the camcorder to videotape the scene.

Even Joe had to duck as he stepped into the little adobe. He stood there awhile as his eyes made the slow transition from brilliant summer sunlight to murky gloom. The morning air outside was approaching 100 degrees. In this dark, stuffy room with its windows closed, the temperature felt like 120. Tom moved in beside him. His smokey-light eyes usually adjusted more quickly than did Joe's. The camcorder hummed as it panned the room.

The normal accoutrements of a semipermanent camp crowded against the walls—to the right of the doorway, a Coleman stove on a wooden table, milk crates and ammo cases no doubt used for temporary food storage, square tin pails with dented lids. The plastic dishpan lay upside down under the stove table. Another larger wooden table on the far wall held bottles and jars, arcane scientific equipment, and cartons. Three snake sticks and a butterfly net leaned against the wall.

To the left, two camp mattresses on iron cots crowded against the wall. If the cots were six feet long, the room was barely more than twelve feet square. Joe could see nothing unusual for a setup of this sort.

As his eyes adjusted better, he took a good close look at the floor. Of beaten earth, it was so claypan hard it yielded no tracks.

Tommy started around the room to the left, clockwise from the door. "It never ceases to amaze me the lengths these folk go to, just to cavort with reptiles. Ever read *Dragons of Eden* by Carl Sagan?"

"No."

"Talks about a primal fear of reptiles programmed right into the deepest regions of our brains. Mr. Bill-yuns-and-Bill-yuns Sagan believes the fear comes from our prehuman reptile or early-mammal ancestors fearing the dinosaurs themselves, before man and monkey ever came to be. That the deepest part of our brain be reptilian or very early mammal in character."

"Where do you get this stuff, Tommy?"

"Gretch was into Sagan for a while there. Some fascinating stuff, actually."

Joe glanced at Tommy. The Irishman was pausing, studying the ground, lost in thought. Or memories. Joe said nothing.

In the far corner sat a makeshift wooden cabinet. A peg in a hasp held its rickety upper door shut. Probably more scientific equipment and bottles. Joe pulled the peg and tried to yank the hasp open. Rust gripped it, kept it from working smoothly. By jerks he halfway opened the creaky door when...

Lightning fast, a gray blur out of the cabinet's darkness flew at Joe's face. It hit his right forearm only because the arm was in its way. Joe yelled, his knees buckled in shock, and he landed heavily. The gray snake dropped to the ground two feet from Joe's navel, flopped about righting itself, and arched into a vicious S-coil, poised to strike again.

Its tail buzzed, dry and shrill.

Joe sat frozen, as much from horror as from wisdom. The snake's head with its flicking tongue swayed slightly, mesmerizing him. Motionless. Joe must remain absolutely motionless. Then the snake flew sideways a foot as Tom's gun roared. It contorted itself instantly into a churning knot. Joe dropped back onto his spine and rolled away. He snapped around to his knees to see where the snake was going, but it writhed in a ball where it had stopped, coiling tortuously in and out of itself. The gun went off again and the snake jerked another six inches away from them.

Tommy dropped down to his knees beside Joe, absolutely paper white, and stammered something unintelligible. His gun, clamped in a death grip, waved about. Then he seemed to gather himself back in by deep breaths and slow degrees until his shaking hands could at last holster his gun.

Joe could feel exactly where the snake had hit, about three inches below his right elbow. He wrapped his fingers tightly around his right arm above the elbow and squeezed.

Tom took a deep breath, and another. At length, the old cool-and-in-command Irishman returned. He popped out his pocketknife.

Joe shook his head. His voice faltered. "Cut-and-suck went out with the stagecoach. I need your shoelace there."

Without hesitation Tom untied his shoe. "And methought tourniquets went out with crossbows."

"Not a tourniquet; a ligature. A tourniquet cuts off all the circulation. A ligature just slows it down a little. Hand tightened." Joe tried to analyze what he felt at the bite site. He shook his head. "Wait."

"What?"

"There's no real deep burning sensation; just the sort of little surface burn pain you'd feel if you scuffed it."

Tom tipped the arm up and frowned. "There should be two fang marks, aye? Red dots as well as tiny scratches?"

"Just scratches?" Joe climbed to his feet and was surprised at how shaky he felt. He staggered over to the doorway and leaned on the jamb. He tilted his arm into the sunlight and let Tommy have a close look.

"No fang marks that I can see."

"None I can feel. But he hit me solid, Tommy."

"Aye. I heard the slap."

"No discoloration." Joe watched his arm in fascination, half expecting it to drop off or something. His sweat made the scuff marks burn. Nothing more. At length he shifted his gaze, sagging against the door frame to stare at Tommy. Tommy stared back at him.

Joe lurched erect and walked back into the middle of the room, his night vision shot again. "Could be another in that cabinet. Wait until your eyes are back before you look."

Tommy stopped in the middle of the floor. "What makes yourself think I'm the one to look?" He dropped down to tie his shoe.

"I took my turn." Cautiously Joe crossed to the rattler. It still squirmed in ugly jerks, but not so violently. He waited until the head flopped out across the dirt floor to bring his boot hard down on it. For the first time since the strike, he let his fingers loosen from his arm. Very carefully he wrapped them around the snake's neck. He worked them up the neck until he could feel the bulge of the jaw. He had to tip his boot sole slightly to grip up closer. Holding his breath, he lifted his foot away.

He stood erect, picking the snake up by that grip on its neck. The snake convulsed suddenly and Joe almost let go of it. The lower two-thirds of the thing fell away and plopped in the dirt; Tommy's bullets had nearly severed the body and its flailing weight in midair completed the job.

"Meself be muckle close to throwing up, me doughty partner. I trust ye know that."

"Me too. Splendid piece of shooting, Tommy. Perfectly placed under impossible conditions. Your pocketknife?" Joe carried the hideous third to the doorway.

Tommy moved in beside him. "I cannot imagine meself doing this thing. 'Tis against me deepest nature. An Irishman. Snakes. St. Patrick knew what he was about when he drove every f'looting one of 'em into the sea. This whole case has given me a set of the willies ye wouldn't believe."

Joe slipped the knife blade into that reptilian gray-pink mouth. He twisted it, prizing the jaws open wide. Then he tilted the diamond head back.

"Begorra," Tom purred. "I can see where those fangs ought to be in its upper jaw there. They cannot retract them, aye? Like a cat's claws?"

"No. The fangs lie flat when the mouth is closed. They can withhold venom, but when they open their mouths, the fangs lock into position automatically."

No fangs. Wire cutters or nippers of some sort had clipped them off or pulled them; Joe couldn't tell which.

Suddenly, totally drained, Joe let himself slide to sitting down on the rough wooden door frame. He tossed his handful of fangless snake over toward where the rest of it lay, closed his eyes, and let his head rest against the weathered wood. Every screaming nerve in his body writhed like that snake. *What primal fear of reptiles, what terror of Sagan's* Dragons of Eden *do Ruth and those others have to quell in order to work among these creatures?*

He heard jars clank and turned to look. In the gloom inside, Tommy was pouring something into a mayonnaise jar. Its aroma wafted Joe's way. Alcohol. Tommy dropped the severed top end into the preserving fluid. "We do not need the back part, aye?"

"No. You can tell it's a rattler without the rattle."

"Good. Meself intends to keep the rattle, unless you'd like it as a memento."

"What do you want with it?"

"For the Flaherty Collection of Criminal Curiosities. This be the very rattle of the very snake who bit me partner."

"And lived to tell the tale. What's going on here, Tommy?"

"How long can a snake live in that cupboard?"

"I don't know. Weeks. We also want to find out if they can grow their fangs back, and if so, how long it takes." Joe climbed to his feet. He could not feel less like performing the next chore that had to be done. He dug his flashlight and nightstick out of the jump box in the back of the 'Burb and went back inside. Methodically, foot by foot, he searched the ragged little adobe for whatever might lurk there yet, poking with the baton, shining the light in every corner and crevice. It took ten nerve-racking minutes.

But for one small blob of snake poop, the cabinet stood empty now. Nothing else lived in the cabin save a harmless little gecko under the dishpan and a few bugs and scorpions. Nothing else waited for them.

Joe and Tommy scoured the area of the other building for tracks and they found nothing there. It was no more than a storage closet, a place to stack scrap lumber, a number of what looked to be some sort of snake traps with sliding lids, various crates and boxes, coils of rope and clothesline and fibrous plastic cord, more jars all gray with dust, steel-and-wire-mesh small mammal traps, a whole bucket of plain old rattraps, and some stovewood and newspapers.

They spent an hour videotaping and inventorying the storage shed roughly and the research hut in measured detail, right down to Tommy's final entry: "Snake, speckled rattle (*Crotalus mitchelli*), 1; rear 2/3 less rattle, 7.5' straight back from the door." With Tommy's print kit they lifted a couple dozen clear fingerprints from the jars and dishpan. People had been here recently.

Joe walked around to the back of the building. A mirror hung from a mesquite tree off the corner of the hut, and a washstand stood against the back wall. Bonanza! They documented and retrieved hairs both short and long, where people had shaved and groomed themselves. Joe was beginning to feel very scientific himself.

"In fact," he suggested, as they finally drove away from the scene, "we ought to send Gretch out here with her big guns. Really go over the place."

"To what end?" Tommy reached down by his feet and rapped the jar with the snake third in it. "Except for the rattler in the cabinet, we've found nothing solid, unless tests of the hair samples come up with something intriguing."

"What do you mean, 'except for the snake'? That thing was in there. Waiting. But why?"

"Why defanged, ye mean?"

"Why everything about it."

Tommy grunted and lapsed into thought.

Once he got off the ruts and out to the graded road, Joe tried to start sifting pieces too. He couldn't. That flying snake had destroyed his mental processes.

The memory of that striking gray head . . .

The Conscience of the Post-Feminist

The Vultures' Roost usually hummed with activity as its denizens hunched over computer terminals, typewriters, and telephones. Joe tapped himself another cup of coffee, stirred some sugar into it, and looked around. The Roost, labeled HOMICIDE on the door, was practically empty. In the far corner, Hugh Bartoli hung up his phone, dragged his coat off the back of his chair, called good-bye and strode out the back door. Joe and Tom were the only ones left here.

Joe strolled to his desk, not at all eager to wade through the morass of paper lurking there. His desk faced Tom's.

Tommy was on the phone again. He spent the better part of his life on one phone or another. "Here," he told his receiver, "talk to Joe. I know so little of such things." He pointed to Joe's phone.

"Gretch on line 2. She's back from the field station."

Joe picked it up and punched in the line. "Good Monday. How's it going?"

"Like Monday. Doug and I went out to your field station this morning and went over the place. I hate getting out before dawn."

"Beats driving in the heat."

"True. You guys did all right, for amateurs. We got the same prints you did plus a couple other people. And tire impressions of three vehicles."

"Now to find the tires."

"I leave that to you. I'm a simple lab lackey. Gary Collier was out there–not recently–and two students with senior projects, Corello himself, and at least two people we haven't identified. Nothing on the hair samples yet. Hey, speaking of hair . . ."

Tom's phone rang. He picked it up and broke into a smile.

Joe's attention snapped back to Gretchen. "What?"

"Arsenic. In Corello's hair. He was taking some interesting drugs because of his heart condition–he had a weak heart, you know–and a lot of drugs show up as traces in hair. We were going to match what we found against his prescriptions. Bingo!"

"Bingo indeed. Would he be taking the arsenic himself? As a heart stimulant or strengthener?"

Silence on the other end a moment. "Could be. It's a sort of folk remedy. They say Sherpas take arsenic to increase their stamina at high altitudes. Not something I'm eager to try."

"Think I'll pass too. We'll stop by and pick up the

reports and supplementals in the morning."

"Can't. I won't be here. I'm going over to the U in the morning to get a raw Gila monster venom sample. I'll drop them by your desk this afternoon."

"Okay." Joe would normally have asked Gretchen if she wanted to talk to Tommy again, but these days were not normal. So Joe extended a few pleasantries and hung up.

Tommy was hanging up too. "That be Ruth Houser. I've an appointment with her in two hours, when she's done with her lab class. She talked some about that field station. Vic ruled it with the same iron hand he ruled everything else. Controlled who went out there and what studies they engaged in. Had a couple botany majors doing plant studies, and Gary Collier's working on something to do with . . ." He studied his notes. "*Hadrurus arizonensis*. That's scientific babble for a big hairy scorpion. I had to ask her to spell it."

"But not rattlers."

"No one working on rattlers."

"You didn't mention our fangless foe?"

"Nor shall I. Meself suggests we keep that one under our hats, and see if someone acts antsy or lets something slip."

"I agree. Where you going now?"

Tommy was standing, pushing his chair in, reaching for his tie. "Over to Tempe. The Jones report was signed not by an honest-to-goodness medical examiner but by a lowly sheriff-coroner. I've a meeting with him to talk about it. 'Twill fit in nicely with the Houser appointment to follow."

"Tommy . . ." How should Joe phrase this? "It

looks to me like you're getting in pretty thick with Ruth Houser. Bad policy, cozying up with a murder suspect."

"Cozy? Hardly. Though I aver she's a charmer." Tommy's face softened. "She's the key person in the Corello empire now, Joe, and knows much that we must know. But more than that, she's sore put upon by this whole thing."

"So you're comforting her in her losses."

"Not exactly. Support. Friendship."

"Cozying. I'm urging you to back off. Think about it, please."

"Ye worry too much, old top. Haastuh loo-eego." And away he went, leaving Joe with the paperwork. He stirred through the mess on his desk and thought briefly about adding a medical to it. *Cancel that idea. I'll let my foot drop off before I add to this hooey with all the forms an on-duty medical claim would dump on me.*

His ankle hurt, though. Spending Sunday with his foot propped up on an ice bag had helped a lot. But with the constant use today, it was right back to sore again.

With a sigh he got back to work. Hours of work. Hang, he hated paperwork. Time dragged by like snails on a driveway.

A lithe blond form hovered by his desk. Joe looked up.

Gretchen was looking down. "Joe? Buy me a beer."

"Love to. Five minutes."

She sat down across from him, laid out her additions to his supplementals, and started collating.

"Where is everybody? It seems so quiet around here."

"Mel's in Pennsylvania. He gets back from vacation tomorrow. Harry and Chen and Turk are all on annual leave till next week. Janet James and two others that I know of are out with that summer crud."

"That twenty-four-hour stomach flu thing? We got two people out with it in the lab."

"Purley says Robbery has a couple out too. Jerry says he's going to close down the division and rent the Homicide room to boiler-room telephone solicitors."

He gathered and Gretchen stapled and together they finished the supplemental in six minutes, within sixty seconds of estimate. Joe laid a copy on Tommy's desk, filed another, and stuffed the third in Jerry's box on the way out.

He walked with her down the back stairs to the rear lot to his Midget. He would have held the car door for her, but she climbed in without thinking about it.

In fact, she was doing everything without thinking about it, it seemed, her eyes and her mind in a vague, distant haze. They rode in silence the twenty blocks to Chico's Rincon.

At this time of day Joe could park near the entrance. She waited for him now, and let him open the car door for her.

She whipped long, lean legs out and stood up. "This is your favorite place, isn't it."

"I don't have any choice. Chico's my cousin."

"Old family recipes?" She led the way to the big

entrance portico.

"Yeah, some of them." He escorted her inside. The hostess was new.

"Buenas tardes!" The girl snatched up two menus. "Smoking or nonsmoking?"

"Table 17 or 28, whichever's open. A draft beer for Gretchen here, a Pepsi no ice for me, and nachos. We don't need the menu." When your cousin owns the place, and you yourself own some of the stock, you can take a few liberties.

"Make that two Pepsis," Gretchen amended. "Lots of ice in mine."

The girl looked blank for only a moment, then pasted on the smile again. "This way, please."

Table 28 was available. Good. Tucked in a quiet corner, it provided privacy and intimacy. The beverage hostess brought the drinks in a matter of moments, announced that the nachos would arrive eventually, and disappeared.

Joe stared across the table at Gretch and held her eye. "Unload. What's going on with you two, anyway?"

Her eyes flitted away. "I don't know, Joe. I wish I knew. I guess it's me."

"Tommy seems confused about the whole thing. And angry."

"He is. He oughta be. It's me." She looked at Joe. "You wouldn't understand because you don't sleep around. You date now and then, but . . . "

"Marie and I are getting serious. That's pretty much it."

"You've known her three months. I'm talking about the last two or three years. I've always had a man. Before Maynard it was Gregg. And, of course, Tommy these last few months. Always somebody. I don't feel complete without a boyfriend, you know? And yet, I'm better off without them. Here I am, the classic post-feminist who doesn't need a man, and I've always got one."

Joe mulled over what he'd just heard. "Post-feminists don't have consciences. That's not really what's eating you."

She laughed suddenly. It burst out of her. "I love it! Post-feminists don't have consciences. Wait'll I tell Fel that. And Lauri. And Grace. They'll stick a rattler in your mailbox." The mirth faded. "Yeah. I'm getting a conscience. Ever look up *fornicator* in the Bible?"

"Not specifically."

"It's always listed with liars and murderers and that ilk—people on the other side of the fence from us cops. Did you know drug dealers and drug users are in the Bible?"

"No. Where?"

"Same places. Mostly in Revelation, where it uses *pharmaceia* and some derivatives. The translators rendered it as sorcery—the secondary usage—but the primary meaning is drug users and dealers."

"So how come the translators didn't just tell it like it is?"

She shrugged. "I suppose, years ago, who'd guess drugs would be the big thing? But sorcery's always been around. Seemed the way to go at the time, I guess." She sipped her Pepsi. "There it is, Joe, the front page of the newspaper, right in Revelation. People who use or deal drugs are named in the same breath with the murderers and fornicators and adulterers."

"Where'd you get all this?"

"I've been studying some." She sighed. "Too much, as far as Tommy's concerned."

"As I recall, you won't have anything to do with married men. You steer clear of adultery. Respect the marriage bond."

"That's right. But there's still the fornication. Anyway, I cut Tommy off. To be more accurate, I cut off me. No more, at least until I can sort out what's going on in my head."

"Guilt?"

"Guilt."

"What's next? Can you see anything down the road?"

"That's what has me scared, Joe. I tried to explain to Tommy, but he just doesn't understand. I think I lost him."

The nachos arrived. Joe waited until the waitress left. "He cares about you very much."

"Did you happen to notice how he acts around that little Houser snippet?"

Joe sighed. How much should he say? The fact that he sensed an even more intense attraction between Tommy and Ruth than Gretchen saw? Or did he? Gretchen was not only sharp at seeing that sort of thing, but she had a vested interest. "Yeah, I noticed."

Gretchen picked at the nachos, but her heart obviously wasn't in it. "I don't know if I'm doing the right thing, Joe. When I went forward and accepted Jesus at Mouse's funeral, I really meant it. Mouse had her act together. I didn't think anything about Tommy and me being lovers; that was neither here nor there. In fact, I didn't really get started in the Bible until a couple weeks ago."

"What set you going?"

"I was talking to that pastor, the one who preached Mouse's funeral. He asked how I was coming along, and I had to tell him that frankly, I wasn't. We talked awhile, and I decided to start reading. Chapter a day in the Bible." She snorted. "You get hooked on that book. I've been reading just about a book a day. Revelation in two days, and then I went back and really looked at it. With a commentary and marginal notes. And every time I reread something, I see more in it."

Joe nodded. "And now Tommy says you've gone fanatical. Off the deep end, and it scares him."

"Exactly." She smiled. "You know him better than he knows himself. That's why I wanted to talk to you. You're on both wavelengths; you understand Tommy and you've committed your life to Christ. Do you see what I should do?"

Joe pondered the problem a few minutes. Good nachos. At length he put his thoughts into words, the better to know what he was thinking. "Sounds like you've got a no-win situation. Hang onto Tommy and you tee off God. Lose Tommy trying to please God and you might be cutting yourself off from your best chance at happiness in the future."

"Yeah. That's it exactly. I really care about Tommy, Joe. I love him."

"Tell you what. I'll recast the situation so she doesn't know it's you I'm talking about, but I'll ask

Marie about it. I'll call her tonight. See what she has to say."

"Go ahead and use my name. Hell, it's my problem." She made a face. "Sorry. That's something else I'm trying to clean up. Language. You know, Joe, this trying to be pious is a real drag."

Someday My Prints Will Come

Around and around it went, under the light on the turntable in her microwave, rotating. Last night's leftover beef tortellini and hash browns from the night before that. Breakfast.

Gretchen watched her repast heat up as she punched in the VARI number on the phone. She got put on hold by two different desk jockeys, one of them that department secretary, Miss Watkins, before she finally reached the Collier kid.

"Collier."

"Gretchen Wiemer, with the forensics lab at—"

"Of course! You stopped by for that tox lit. Blond, beautiful, about five eight or nine."

"Flattery will get you anywhere. We talked about your getting me a sample of Gila monster venom this morning. Is that still on?"

"Sure. I'll bring it in to you if you want. Lyophilized. It's stable, doesn't need refrigeration."

"Good. But I also want a sample fresh from the lizard, the way it would be introduced by a bite. Can I get some fresh milk?"

"I'll milk one before your very eyes, if you like. You ought to come over here for that, though. All the equipment's here."

"How long does it stay stable outside the lizard?"

"I assume you'll be using it right away?"

"Within hours."

"No problem. Tell me when and I'll be waiting." The kid sounded just plain eager.

"Half an hour?"

"It'll take you that long to find a parking place. Let's make it forty-five minutes. Basement, west wing."

Gretchen laughed. "You're a practical man, Mr. Collier."

"Mr. Collier is my father. I'm Gary."

"See you in forty-five minutes, Gary; sooner, if I can find a parking spot."

It took less than five minutes to eat her breakfast. She scooped up her bag of tricks and left for the U immediately. Gary was right; it took her forty-five minutes, what with the parking. She ended up putting her car in a stadium lot and hoofing it to the VARI facility.

She jogged down the outside stairwell of the building and shoved through doors heavy enough to prevent snakes from escaping, or students, or rhinoceroses. A blast of arctic air practically shoved her right back out. West wing. This was not an area of the building through which Houser had led her. She tried to orient herself as best she could and ended up simply reading signs on doors—and Far Side cartoons—until she found an open door with Gary Collier inside.

So this was the infamous cage room. She paused to look around. The cages and layout were just as Doug's and Joe's reports described them. She crossed to the big glass cage with all the Gila monsters.

She stooped to peer in eye to eye with the lizards. "Such pretty things, when you look at them subjectively. Hello, Gary."

"Even if you look at them objectively. The world's only known venomous lizard family, and only two species in the family. Unique scalation seen nowhere else. Unique physiognomy. Innocuous. For all their poison, they don't go around looking for trouble." He grinned like a high school kid. "Hello, Gretchen. Well," he rubbed his hands together, "let's do it."

He lifted the plywood lid. His hand hovered over the fat, sluggish lizards. It plunged downward, then jerked upward. He had a Gila monster by the top of its neck. It dangled, its stubby black legs waving helplessly. He removed it from the case. It turned out to be a mild-mannered old fellow who didn't feel like biting anything.

"Any way of knowing exactly which lizard was out loose beside the body?"

"Sure, but it'll take a minute. Do you remember the number?"

Gretchen searched her memory. She'd read Joe's

prelims and even remarked on the incongruity of numbering lizards. "Does 156 ring a bell?"

"Sounds right." He picked up lizards and she read off numbers until they got to 156. It looked exactly like all the others. Gary gripped it expertly around the neck and body, one-handed. He began teasing the lizard, threatening it with a finger, literally poking it on its nose.

"This makes as much sense as those signs in national parks that tell you, 'Don't molest the bears,' " Gretchen commented. "Who in his right mind molests a bear? Or a poisonous lizard?"

"I guess I do." Gary chuckled. "You know they don't have fangs. The only way they can introduce their venomous saliva is by chewing on the victim, working the spit in. Most researchers will say they don't think the monster uses its venom at all for predation."

"I've heard that all those tales about people dying from Gila monster bites are myth. Fiction."

"Not only that, their teeth come out real easy. Not rooted. If you have a lizard chewing on you and you don't just grab it by the tail and yank it off, you're too stupid to live anyway."

It didn't take but a moment to get the lizard riled enough to clamp onto a piece of polymer with its strange little teeth.

"We used to just use a piece of black rubber for this." Gary tugged on the polymer sheet, got the lizard to chew and shift its grip. "Switched to this because it's inert."

"And black rubber is ert, right?"

Gary laughed. "To an extent, yeah. Not as clean

as we'd like."

Gretchen drew off its saliva with a capillary tube as Gary worked the lizard. They eventually filled half a small vial.

Gary straightened. "That's about it. If we were lyophilizing this we'd rinse the sheet off to get the last of it. I assume you don't want this diluted at all."

"Right. As is is sufficient, right here. I really appreciate this, on behalf of the department."

"How about personally?" He was looking at her steadily.

She considered a moment, then smiled. "Only at a professional level. I'm spoken for." And she felt a curious mix of elation and embarrassment at the thought.

"Too bad. We could get together later. It'd be fun. Rodriguez? Or that redhead who mentioned you a few times. The Irishman?"

"No. Jesus."

She left the cage room with venom both fresh and lyophilized in her bag of tricks. Gary Collier's prints she had. She also had all the seniors and grad students associated with the lab, the deceased—Corello and Craig both—the Houser snippet, but not the Houser dad or Lowry. She worked her way over to the part of the quadrangle she knew and sought out Dr. Osada's office.

The door stood open. She knocked.

"Come."

The quiet, elegant Dr. Philip Osada sat in the back room of a totally filled two-room cubicle, pecking energetically at a computer keyboard. His monitor displayed an elaborate graph in full living color.

"Gretchen Wiemer, Phoenix forensics lab."

He stood up. "Of course. You were present Friday morning, plying your trade out in the compound. You whisked Mr. Houser away as smoothly as I've ever seen him whisked."

She laughed. "I apologize for bothering you. There's a routine matter I have to take care of, and I was over here anyway . . . " She let her voice trail off.

"Ah, routine. Were it not for routine, we could do such great things."

"Ain't it the truth!" Gretchen set her bag on a pile of papers because there was no uncluttered surface in this room. "We need fingerprints from everyone associated with VARI."

He froze momentarily. Gretchen could feel the instant chill. Then he warmed again, just as quickly. "Fingerprints. Of course." He smiled. "Somehow we who know nothing of modern police methods get the impression that science has moved beyond old-fashioned fingerprints."

"Not at all. They're a hotter ticket than ever. It will take less than five minutes. May I roll yours now? Or should I make an appointment?"

"Let us do it now and we're both done with that bit of routine."

"I appreciate this very much, Dr. Osada." She whipped out her kit and set up as quickly as she could. She maintained a light patter to keep him loose. He cooperated well, but he clearly had never done this before. With more light, cheerful words, she closed down her kit, laid the sheet carefully in the top of her bag until the ink dried well, and excused herself.

Now for the coffee room. She found it again on the first pass. What looked like the same cardboard sheet of doughnuts sat there beside the urn. She looked around . . . no one in sight. She grabbed the whole batch of sugar packets in one big handful and stuffed them in her purse. She put down her bag of tricks and began systematically going through cupboards, taking samples.

She had taken dust samples from all but one of the cupboards and sideboards when Dorothy Stearns came trotting in. The lady's round face erupted in a warm, spontaneous smile. "I remember you . . . the young lady who twisted Jason Houser around her little finger. Good morning. Are you looking for something?"

"Sugar." Gretchen grinned. "I was going to get some coffee, but there's no sugar." She waved a hand toward the empty sugar-packet container.

"Of course." Mrs. Stearns dropped down to one knee and opened a lower cupboard. "Here we go. Are you here on business or just looking around?" She dug out a wad of sugar packets.

"Business. In fact, you're one of the people I need. I'm taking fingerprints of everybody in the place. Didn't get yours yet."

Mrs. Stearns stood up with a dark and puzzled look. "That means you think I—" she let the thought hang.

"It doesn't mean that at all. It means that if we find a suspect and take him to court, the defense will try to get him off by claiming the investigation was incomplete, so we make sure it's not incomplete. Every case we handle, we get a sheaf of useless paper this high." She gestured.

"Mmm." She jammed the sugar into the container. "Well, I suppose . . . if you have to do it. Seems rather silly to me."

"It's like when you're painting a lawn chair." Gretchen surreptitiously put away her dust samples and got out her print kit. "You paint the underside too, even though no one's going to see it."

Mrs. Stearns smiled suddenly, the doubts apparently past. "You do have an interesting job."

"Sometimes, yes. Now just relax and let me do all the work. Don't try to help me." She gripped Dorothy's hand and rolled the index finger. Dorothy tried to help.

Gretchen got another sheet. "Let's try again. No, let's practice on this smudged one first and then do it for real on the clean one. You'll get the hang of it with practice." She rolled the middle finger. "For instance, yesterday I went out to Dr. Corello's field station. You ever been out there?"

"The passion pit? No."

Gretchen stopped and frowned at her. She smiled suddenly. "The passion pit, huh?"

"Oh, my, yes! Not that all the students who go out there go for—you know, prurient reasons. But Dr. Corello would turn up there every now and then unannounced—sneaking around is the only way to say it—and on one occasion he caught two students, uh, how do you say it?"

"In flagrante delicto?"

"That's it!"

"So he was always out there nosing around, you might say."

"He never trusted anybody."

Gretchen set the clean sheet in the clip. "Okay, you're doing well. Just do it the way we have been." She rolled the index finger. Good one. "Tell you what. I won't ask nosy questions, but I'll bet you know all the couples in the department . . . who's going with whom."

"I consider it my job. Many of the students confide in me. They tell me their troubles. Many of them have no one else to talk to. It's very sad . . . away from home, or on the outs with the parents, or the parents simply too busy."

"I'm glad." Three fingers done. "I'm thinking of people like Ruth Houser, for instance, and her father. No way she could tell that man her problems. Especially love problems. I'm glad she has someone like you."

"Exactly." Mrs. Stearn wagged a wizened head. "Ruth. She's such a lovely girl, and she has such terrible luck with romantic involvements."

"I know *that* feeling."

Tommy.

"We all do, of course. But when you're Ruth's age, a romantic misadventure becomes a catastrophe. And she's had more than her share of shocks and losses."

"What do you mean? Here, relax your fingers. That's right."

"Why, look at her track record, so to speak. Dr. Corello. I don't know that he was a romantic figure in her life, but he was a father figure. An important part of her life and career. Gone. And she had such a lovely relationship with the Craig boy. Again, I don't mean romantic. At least, I don't think so. I mean close companionship. And the Jones boy. They were such a darling couple, she and Jonesy."

"Jones. Oh, that's right. The fer-de-lance a year and a half ago. Now the thumbs. Keep it loose. That's right."

"But then, Ruth is very open to just about everyone in the department. She has no enemies. No matter who died—Phil, John, me myself even—it would be someone she knew well."

"But she and Jonesy weren't what you'd actually call an item, were they? Here's a towelette. Wipe your fingers off on that and then wash them. Should all come right off."

"You know, I sometimes wonder about that. I rather think they were, Ruth and Jonesy—an item, I mean. Such a darling couple. Perfect for each other."

"Well, certainly not my business. I'm a lab tech, so I don't do interrogations or anything. Besides, it doesn't pertain to the business at hand, you know?"

"Of course." Dorothy carefully, methodically, wiped her fingers off. "I'm sure someday Ruth's prince will come—someone she can truly call her own. She so deserves a fine young man."

Just so long as her prince isn't Tommy. The thought of it wrenched at Gretchen.

Dorothy was still smiling. "Do you have other people to fingerprint?"

"No more here at VARI. I got Dr. Osada a few

minutes ago."

"Phil." Dorothy nodded. "Such a conscientious, careful man. I value good conscience in a researcher. There's an important place for live animal research. But beyond a certain ethical line there is no place for it. Phil never crosses that line."

Gretchen packed up the last of her stuff. "Joe said you're a strong advocate for animals."

"Not a fanatic. Vic called me a fanatic and that's not true. Like I say, there's an important place for live animal research. But when it shouldn't be happening, I'll fight it with every weapon I have."

"Joe says you fought Corello bitterly."

"But I couldn't break the system. I'm very sorry to say this, because it sounds like I'm balancing Vic's life against the lives of a bunch of white rats. But a lot of senseless suffering and slaughter stopped when he died."

Gretchen asked softly, "Are you glad?"

The lady held her eye a few moments. "I'm ashamed to say it, but in a way I am. That's terrible, but it's true."

Gretchen grinned and extended her hand for a shake. "Do you realize how wonderful it is to talk to someone who has the guts to face ugly realities and deal with them? I admire your honesty, Mrs. Stearns, very much. God bless you!"

Dorothy seized Gretchen's hand in both of hers. "And God bless you, dear."

Gretchen took her leave and walked back to the car. She'd better get this Gila monster venom back to the lab.

And God bless you, dear. And God bless you,

Gretchen. No one had ever called God's blessing down on her that way before, and it lifted her spirits far more than she would expect of such a thing.

God bless you, dear.

And God bless you, Tommy. I love you. But I have to do it God's way.

She cried all the way back to town.

Winning Ways

Ruth Houser stood in the doorway of the first floor east lecture room, watching students file out. There ought to be a law against summer sessions, particularly in Arizona, where summer burns with such vengeance. These people were all so dull, so drained, so lackadaisical. Students these days were pitifully nonscholarly anyway. Adding the heat of midsummer to their natural inertia produced zombies. Ruth hated summer sessions. She absolutely hated them.

Here came a man who was the antithesis of dull, drained, and lackadaisical. Tom Flaherty came rollicking down the hall toward her. *Rollicking* was the only way to describe his snappy gait with the elbows flapping, the perpetually disheveled hair bouncing.

She turned out the lecture hall lights. "Good evening, Tom."

"Top of the evening, lass. Might I escort ye to your office?"

"Please do." Ruth started down the hall and he fell in beside her. So floppy and loose a moment ago, he tightened up, so to speak. He walked firmly, purposefully. He had turned into her escort. What a curious transformation!

"Did ye talk to your papa at all yet?"

"I learned long ago that I can avoid him for a while, but it doesn't pay to hide for too long. I went home this weekend. He was livid the whole two days, lecturing me about how it looks for a church deacon's daughter to be mixed up in a murder."

"Not to mention the snakes in question."

"He should be used to them by now. Snakes are my stock in trade."

"Why?"

"What?"

"Why did ye choose snakes, of all things, for a life's work?"

"They appeal to me. They have such a rich history, and a fascinating mythology. Different cultures, different myths and attributes. If you'll excuse the pun, men and snakes are intertwined through all our days. But actually, my doctorate's in certain aspects of venination, not the snakes per se."

"And I still cannot perceive exactly how Vic Corello's death endangered your degree work."

She sighed heavily at the very thought. "You know how physicists are looking for a Grand Unifying Theory? A GUT they call it, to tie all their present theories together. Well, Vic was certain he had a GUT about venom in animals." She pushed the elevator button.

"Tying together all the diverse ways of poisoning that critters employ?"

"Oversimplified a bit, but that's basically it. He had four of us working on different parts of his GUT." She stepped into the elevator. Tom stepped in beside her. She hit the 4 button. "Obviously, he had it all in his head. He knew where he wanted our work to go, and then he'd tie the ends together in a big bow and earn himself some more laurels."

"And yourselves would share those laurels by virtue of your various contributions. Your participation."

"That's right." She sighed again. "At least that was the idea."

"Doesn't your grant request specify what ye should be doing? Meself always thought grants were awarded for specific projects with specific ends."

"If you read the grant proposals individually, none of them really frames a coherent project." The elevator dipped to a halt. She slapped the door three times to make it open and headed out and down the hall. "They were apparently intended as a unit, a group. But when you put them all together, no matter how you mix and match them, you can't get anything out of them. We can't figure out what he was thinking. Only Phil has anything like a stand-alone project, and he wasn't really interested in Vic's ideas. The only reason he pursued his project was that the rest of us needed his work for everything to come out. The *Tantillas* were primary in his life, not Vic's work."

"Who specifically would lose?"

She waved her key ring. "Have you ever seen so many keys? I have this theory that a person's importance is inversely proportional to the number of keys she carries. The big boss carries maybe one or two master keys. All the rest of us peons carry tons of them."

Tom laughed heartily. "A telling truism, lass!"

She sorted out her office key and jammed it in the lock. "I lost this key ring once, for a week. What a nightmare! We thought we were going to have to change all the locks in the building. They had extra security here every night."

"Where'd ye find it?"

"At home. I came home the next Friday after school and Dad tossed them on the table at supper and said, 'Did you miss these?' 'Why didn't you call me and tell me you had them?' I yelled. 'I came across them yesterday, and you were coming home today, and I was busy,' he said, and as far as he was concerned, that ended it." She swung her office door open. "Come in, please."

She crossed to her side chair, flopped into it and pulled her shoes off, utterly weary. "Who would lose? John Lowry, a lot. Phil Osada, a little. Me, everything. Gary Collier, quite a bit. And if the big shuffle materialized, everyone."

"Big shuffle?" When Tom relaxed, parts of him flowed all over. He sat down in the secondhand, overstuffed armchair her father used when he came in to visit. His arms draped over the sides, one lanky leg sprawled forward, and the other looped over the arm.

"Vic was going to restructure the department. Bring in new blood, he called it."

"How severely restructure?"

"Top to bottom. Reassign existing personnel to other areas, get rid of the volunteer program altogether and hire—"

"Get Dorothy Stearns out?"

"Yes. And build a new department devoted, essentially, to Vic Corello studies."

"He had the muscle to perpetrate all this?"

"Especially if he got his video finished, he would. The University let him have anything he wanted. He was very popular—I mean with the popular media as opposed to the scientific literature. We have a public broadcast studio right here on campus, you know. He was going to sign a contract to launch a series with them."

Tom's expressive eyebrows popped up. "Sort of the Carl Sagan of venomous animals?"

"What Joseph Campbell did for myth and Carl Sagan did for the universe. Right."

"Mmm." Tom mulled all this a few moments. "We've been discussing these nasty things your boss was wont to do. But sure and he had to have good points, for the University to back him so, aye? His winning ways?"

"Winning ways. Yes. Some wonderful strengths." Through Ruth's memory flashed so many little vignettes of Vic, the scenes the rest of the world knew nothing about, and those thoughts nearly brought tears to her eyes. His death hurt so badly. "Proud. Determined. Resourceful. You know how Captain Bligh got dumped off the *Bounty,* so he sailed in a rowboat how many thousand miles?"

"An incredible feat of seamanship, aye. A superb officer."

"If we mutinied and put Vic in a rowboat, so to speak, he would come through like that. Achieve the impossible. He had the iron will to get whatever he felt was needed. An iron will is a very positive attribute in a man. In any person. He was a survivor. That's positive too. And yet, Vic was actually quite tender and pleasant, one on one. Not in public, but in private. And a showman. A wonderful showman."

"All show, no substance?"

"Just the opposite! Plenty of substance. But he . . . " She stopped. She threw away the words she would have used and substituted others. "Americans don't care very much about things that are totally remote. Two hundred thousand people die in a Bangladesh monsoon and we give it some lip service, offer up a couple prayers in church, and that's it. But let one American die in a monsoon and it's a killer storm. Well, Vic brought venomous animals to the public consciousness. He gave them a voice and a face."

"People care about what they know and see. The familiar. Aye." Tom nodded vigorously. "And your Vic served those animals by helping people learn about them and therefore care."

"Exactly!" Ruth sat forward in her seat. "Like Cousteau. No scientific papers have ever been published out of his *Calypso* studies. But he uses big, colorful coffee-table books, and videos and movies to make the oceans familiar to Americans—to everyone in the world—and now when oceans are threatened, people care."

"The same thing Disney did with his True Life Adventures. Before Disney, animal predators were bad guys. After Disney, they were a welcome and important part of nature."

Ruth nodded happily. "Yes! You see!" Tom Flaherty was such a bright and clever man, so quick to catch the thread of what you were thinking, whether you expressed it well or not. Ruth did not consider herself very articulate, but Tom picked up her thoughts and recast them clearly.

"Where would yourself be in his restructuring? Did he discuss it with ye?"

"I was the only one guaranteed a position in the new department. He had me set up for post-doc, then a staff position."

"Mm." Tom stared at her desk a few moments. "And why would he guarantee yourself a position and no one else? Everyone else seemed worried they'd be given the boot."

"I'm a woman. These days, if there are five ranking candidates for a university position, or even a dozen, and one of them is a woman, she will get it. I suppose it's not fair to males, especially white males, but hiring procedures were unfair to females for hundreds of years. We're finally catching up. Vic was bowing to the flavor of the times, you might say."

"Did he share yours and your father's faith?"

"You mean religion?" She snorted. How should she say this so as not to offend him? He might be very religious. His partner seemed to be. "No. Vic was agnostic, though he didn't tell Daddy that."

"And what are you?"

"Nothing." Ruth grinned on the inside. Tom could not possibly know how freeing that simple one-word response was. Nothing.

At last, no investment in the church she was forced to attend almost daily as she was growing up. The choir, because Daddy wanted his daughter in the choir. Children's church. Worship. Sunday night service. Midweek prayer meeting. Youth group. Sunday School. The constant potlucks and hayrides and car washes and retreats and World This Day and World That Day and Vacation Bible School and the endless holiday preparations and observances, all so that Daddy would look good in the church. She had to participate in them all. All.

We don't see you in youth group anymore, Ruth. Why don't you come to youth group? I'm not a youth anymore, thank you very much. We don't consider you a woman, either, Ruth. Why don't you marry, and then we'll let you feel welcome in the women's group? The constant talk of hellfire and damnation, and what proper young ladies ought to wear and what they ought to say and not say, so that Daddy could look good. It was all behind her. All over. Nothing.

Tom seemed not the least put off that she didn't profess a strong faith. He lurched forward in his chair. "Me dear, 'tis near enough dinnertime, we ought be discussing these matters over a steak. Shall we repair to a restaurant? Me treat."

"I'd love it. But we'll have to stop by the cage room on the way out. Is that all right?" She slipped into her shoes.

"Certainly!" He bounded to his feet. She dug her purse out of the bottom drawer of her desk and hooked the strap over her shoulder. She turned out the light and locked the door behind them. She noticed that he had learned how to work the elevator with its eccentric door problem.

They chatted all the way down to the cage room, and Ruth couldn't have told you what the subject was. Tom was too distracting. She could feel his presence beside her, his energy and his closeness. She unlocked the cage room and stepped inside. He entered behind her. She closed the door and shot the inside bolt, but she did not turn on the light.

In the thick darkness of this windowless room, among the snakes, she instantly drew his face down to hers. She kissed him, and it wasn't a sisterly peck, either. He was startled, even say dumbfounded, but he recovered quickly enough. His arms wrapped about her almost immediately, and he returned the kiss in kind. These first kisses were all alike.

She must not let him take what all men sought to take, given half a chance. Absolutely not. She was a good girl. She must break away, run away from this, escape. She abandoned the kiss and nibbled his ear.

He lifted away for a moment to gaze on her, unseeing in the blackness. He cupped both long, bony hands around her face and drew her into another kiss. It was a tender one this time, sweet and lingering. She had never been kissed by someone this tall. She had to stand on extreme tiptoe, and even so, they both cricked their necks. Tom was so tall; Vic had been just right.

It was going to happen again. She was evil before, and she was going to be evil now, and she had no strength of purpose, no powerful will, with which to resist.

She thought of all the rooms in darkness and all the arms around her. They were all alike and they were all different. Vic was different. So was this.

She mustn't let him get away with anything. She must be firm. This must stop! If he wanted to burn in hell, that was his affair. But she must not let him force her into wrongdoing like this. This was all his fault! He started to lift away again but she quickly drew him back.

If ever her father found out about this, what would he do?

Green, Green

Experience England for yourself. And further into the flyer, *Two thousand years of recorded history is only the tip of the iceberg.* Joe put the sales pitch aside and picked up the library book on his desk. Published in Great Britain, it described in the detail typical of a trail guide just what you would do and see as you hiked among the Yorkshire Dales around Harrogate. The countryside charmed him, although he noted that very few of the photos included a really blue sky or sharply defined shadows. Alien country, alien climate, alien creatures. Intriguing.

Reginald and Beatrice Waite—parents of Joe's late wife, Louise, and Rico and Glo's grandparents. He corresponded with them fairly regularly, of course, but had never met them. They lived near Bedford, north of London. John Bunyan country. *Pilgrim's*

Progress land.

And then, up in Wisconsin, there was Marie.

The phone buzzed, dragging him by one ear back to reality. "Rodriguez."

"This is Doug. What do you think of our little scoop there?"

"What little scoop?"

"Didn't Gretch show you the supplemental?"

"Haven't seen her. Steal her thunder for me, Doug."

"Arsenic. She took some casual samples from the cupboards in the coffee room. Bingo. So I went in with a warrant and went over it proper. We've got solid courtroom evidence that someone was handling arsenic in the coffee room."

"Do tell." Joe's brain smiled. It probably wouldn't be Corello himself. If he were voluntarily taking arsenic, he'd do it in the privacy of his home or, at the very least, in his office. "Someone was doing him in?"

"Escalating doses, judging from his hair. No arsenic on the premises now, but the perp would surely get rid of it the minute Corello keeled over of other causes. Flush the evidence."

"Literally?"

"We tested toilets. Not conclusive, of course, but we didn't find anything."

Some ideas about this baffling case were beginning to shape themselves in Joe's mind. "And Gretch has the papers?"

"Wherever in the world she is, yeah."

"Beautiful work, you guys."

"There's more. She got some dirt from that Dorothy person that will interest you."

"I'll see if she's over on this side. If she shows up there, tell her I'll buy her dinner if she'll tell me all the dirt."

"She has it all written up in her report."

"Yeah. She's good at keeping her paperwork caught up." Joe couldn't hold the green imps of envy at bay. Gretchen handled paperwork like a quarterback handles a football. Joe fumbled it like a butterfingers. "But I can't ask a supplemental anything. I want to be able to ask questions."

"I'll tell her." Doug wished Joe well and hung up.

Where would Gretchen be on this side? She was doing some work for Robbery and a couple little things for Vice. Joe stuffed a bunch of catch-up work in his briefcase and practically had to sit on it to get it shut. He and Tommy had a lot of writing and filing to do on the Gila monster. He left a note on his desk for Gretchen asking her to wait for him, and went off searching.

Luck struck. He turned the corner around Jerry's office and headed down the hall, and there she was coming toward him. He grinned and started to raise a hand in greeting. He stopped.

Gretchen looked absolutely green. "Joe, get away from me. I'm coming down with that gut-rot. I don't want you to catch it." She ducked aside into the women's room.

Joe stood in the hallway a few minutes contemplating all this. He had enough paperwork in his briefcase right now to keep him busy till midnight. Midnight next week. And he was years behind in his good deeds for the day.

He rapped on the restroom door. "Anybody beside Gretchen in there?"

No answer. He pushed the door open and stepped very cautiously into no-man's-land. "Gretch?"

"Go away."

"You don't plan to drive home in that shape, do you?"

"I don't plan to leave this stall."

"Sooner or later, some janitor is going to want to scrub out the toilet bowl."

"He can work around me."

A minute later the toilet flushed. Joe waited. The latch rattled and she stepped out, looking totally bedraggled.

He held out his hand. "Come on."

Obediently she took it. She leaned on him all the way to the elevators. She melted against him in the elevator. When the lift cruised to a stop, her head bobbed. He pushed the outside door open. The late afternoon heat literally shoved her back.

Joe scooped her up off her feet and carried her out to the Midget, her heels bumping against his briefcase. He set her down in the passenger seat. "Just hang your head over the gunwale if you feel it coming."

"Right." She shuddered.

He pulled out into traffic and slipped into the fast lane. A few blocks on the way to her home, she spoke suddenly. "Joe, I'm sorry. I need a bathroom. Right now. I mean *right now.*"

He glanced back, switched lanes and hung a hard right. His place was a lot closer than hers.

She moaned the classic Anglo-Saxon word for excrement, and in moments he realized she meant that literally. A few tears ran down her cheeks, but they seemed more misery than embarrassment. "Joe, I'm sorry."

"Only apologize for errors over which you have control. This doesn't qualify."

"Joe, no! We're not going to your place. Take me home."

"You need a second pair of hands to keep your ginger ale supply going. Besides, you could get dizzy and fall, with no one around to help. It's not safe."

"Yeah, but you don't understand."

"Yes I do. I've got a nose. You're talking to a man who's changed a thousand diapers. No problem."

"Joe . . . "

"Quitchur bellyaching and just sit back and relax. I've taken over this show."

"Joe . . . " The top end erupted. Tony Bennett lost his heart in San Francisco and Gretchen Wiemer lost her stomach at Thomas and Twenty-Fourth.

He parked in Morry's slot because it was closest to the apartment stairs. He helped her out and made a mental note to wash the Midget tonight. She made it all the way down the hall and into the bathroom before she lost it again. Fortunately it was on the tile floor and not the hall carpet. He stuck her in the bathtub with instructions to strip, yanked the shower curtain closed, and dug out the six-foot beach towels. He grabbed a handful of paper towels in the kitchen and pulled a garbage bag out of the closet for the soiled clothes. Thus armed, he returned to the bathroom.

He stuck the garbage bag behind the shower curtain. "Put your stuff in that and shower." He cleaned up the floor, took the garbage bag with her clothes out to the laundry closet and left them on the washer, and turned down the bed. "I'll be back in five minutes." He took a bucket of water out and washed off the side of the car before the acid ate into his wax job. As he came back in, the shower was turning off.

He handed some beach towels through. "Wrap up."

"Joe, I'm not sure . . . "

"You're welcome to stay in there awhile, or lie down, whatever works best."

She finally stepped out onto the floor all swathed in beach towels and raised her bleary eyes to his. "I appreciate this. You don't know how much I appreciate it. This is so far beyond the call of duty . . . " Her cheeks were the color of bleached celery.

"Go lie down before you fall over."

Wrapped in towels, she shuffled to the bedroom. He tucked her in, towels and all. Then he washed his hands very, very thoroughly.

He raided the fridge and found a container of posole. With cheese and tortillas it should feed two comfortably. He built two tossed salads and left them on the counter. He spread everything in his briefcase out across the table. What a mess. He dreamed in vain of some line of work requiring no paper shuffling. He was assembling his second case jacket when Tommy finally rattled the door. Joe answered it.

Tommy was scowling, his pallid eyebrows scrunched together. "Gretchen's car be still in the lot at work, and the van's not out, but she's gone apparently. Would ye know where she went off to?"

"Yeah. She's in my bed."

Tommy wheeled and stared, and for a brief moment Joe thought the man might explode. Tom made a lunge toward the door but Joe blocked it.

"Go say hello, but don't kiss her. She's got germs."

The eyebrows lifted slightly and wrinkled. Looking perplexed, Tom broke the stare off and headed down the hall. He got halfway when Gretchen came bursting out the bedroom door.

"Get back!" she cried. She barely made it to the bathroom before she lost her stomach again. Joe handed Tommy a fistful of paper towels. "Your turn." He went back to his paperwork. Let the ex-lover clean up the floor and tuck her in this time. When he heard voices in the bedroom he got up and popped a beer from the fridge.

Tom came wandering out into the living room, looking a little dazed. Joe stuffed the beer in his hand. "Sit."

Tom flopped onto the sofa.

Joe settled into the chair across from him. "Talk."

Tommy sat forward suddenly, elbows on knees. Then he snapped back to sprawling on his spine and stared at the ceiling a bit. "I wish I knew. Meself was certain I be done with her. Then yourself said she was in your bed and I was ready to whip out me sidearm and blow your darlin' head off. Sure and I've never been this addled over a lady. She hasn't captured me heart, she's turned it inside out."

"What are you going to do next?"

"Put her behind me. Or so I thought." He shook his tousled head. "I cannot say."

"What about Ruth?"

Tom paused, and in that pause Joe could see the whole truth laid out. *Rats and double rats!* Joe's spirits took a nose dive. Ruth and Tom were intimate. And when Tom was intimate, he was infatuated, and when he was infatuated, he was totally infatuated.

Joe kept his voice quiet. "Gretch's jealous of Ruth, you know."

"She doesn't know anything."

"Wanna bet the ranch on that? I can use a good ranch."

" 'Tis business with Ruth and meself."

"Business and a whole lot more. Don't try to get devious with me, partner."

Tom jerked forward and set his beer untouched on the coffee table. Without a coaster. He leaned his elbows on his knees and buried his face in his hands momentarily. He rubbed his face, inhaled deeply a couple times, stared at the shag rug. " 'Twas not meself ended the friendship with Gretchen. Not me own idea. Ye know that."

"She ended one aspect of it, not the whole friendship. And she did it for the highest of moral reasons—to please God. She still loves you. And apparently, from what we saw just now, you care far more for her than you're willing to admit to yourself."

"But she . . ." Tommy sighed. "Ye know what that means, don't ye, drawn to its logical conclusion? That makes meself jealous of God."

"You always did do everything to extremes."

Tommy stared at Joe a full two seconds. He burst into a raucous Irish laugh. Then he flopped back on his spine and chuckled mirthlessly at the ceiling.

Joe was even happier than Tom that the tension had broken. Time to change the subject, and perhaps return to it later, when Tommy was off guard. "According to Gretch and Doug, someone was slowly poisoning our victim. Arsenic in the coffee room."

"Indeed!" Tommy grew thoughtful. "Let's see. In our conversations, Ruth mentioned that Vic considered it beneath his station to make coffee. She said it with no bitterness. I would say that enough of her father's chauvinist attitudes persist that she accepts coffee-making as a female task, unlike some liberated ladies of the day. She makes coffee the days Dorothy does not come in. Dorothy makes terrible coffee, she says."

"Intrinsically terrible coffee, or coffee that tastes terrible because arsenic is in it?"

Tom lurched to his feet and headed off down the hall. Joe heard his voice and Gretchen's. Time for dinner. Joe torched off the microwave, nuking the leftover posole. He turned on the burner under the iron griddle and got out some tortillas. By the time he was grating the cheese, Tom returned.

Tom pulled two plates down from the cupboard. "Gretch says we're to get hair samples from everyone concerned. If someone's been playing with arsenic, traces might well show up in them. Possibly fingernails as well. Hard to avoid contamination, particularly if ye be an amateur at handling hazardous materials."

"Nearly everyone involved, including Ruth and Dorothy, are trained to handle hazmats. Chemistry techs, if not majors."

" 'Twill take a lot of time, obtaining the necessary warrants and all. I dread taking it."

Joe shoved his papers to one side of the table as Tommy brought the salads and water tumblers. So Tommy didn't want to take the time to explore the arsenic angle. Or did Tommy not want to investigate an angle that might point a finger at Ruth? She made coffee, though no one was exempt; anyone could put a bit of gray powder in someone's cup.

Joe nodded. "I'll foist it off on someone else."

And he knew just where to foist it.

After dinner Tommy ran down to the minimart briefly for more ginger ale for Gretchen and, at her behest, a toothbrush. The two of them shuffled paper until nearly midnight, and still didn't get everything done. Joe spent the night on the sofa. When he left the next morning at 7:30, Gretchen was, for the first time in a day, sleeping peacefully.

Lad and Lady

"Oh come on, Rodriguez! Why *me*? You can find someone else for that."

Joe watched Mel Carter dump a second packet of sugar in his coffee without thinking. Mel did that only when he was upset. "Why *not* you, Mel? I need someone who can schmooze the ladies. And Daddy Houser doesn't trust anyone who doesn't look Nordic. Or at least northern European."

"You have the appropriate search warrants. You don't need a schmoozer. You can bull right in and do it."

"Diplomacy. Tact. Besides, you're good looking. Put together your good looks with your smooth way of working, and you're exactly what we need for this."

Mel snorted. He ran his fingers through his sandy-brown hair and stared morosely at his coffee.

Joe softened his voice. "What's bothering you, Mel? More than my simple request."

Mel glanced at him almost shamefaced and wandered off across the room to the windows. He ran an *aaah* through his nose. "Just the whole stinking thing. Here you are up to your neck in another glamor case. You not only cleared that Persis Magen case—internationally known star of church and television—you get a girl out of the deal. I get a domestic that still isn't cleared. You get that dinosaur case with an internationally known moviemaker and I get that rotten deal up on Bell Road with the possible drug angle. I've drawn three street-people killings in a row. Kill the bum and roll him and leave the mess for Carter to handle."

"Luck of the draw."

"Bull! That's what's got me so ticked. You can't be living *that* right."

How should he handle this? Joe pondered options and figured out pretty quickly that he didn't have many. One of them was honesty, but it was chancy. It was obvious he couldn't predict Mel's response; he hadn't in the least anticipated this spate of jealousy.

He backed up to a window and perched his butt on the sill. "Confession time. I asked you in on this for ulterior motives."

Mel turned slightly to look at him.

Joe pressed on. "You might even get a girl out of the deal. Tommy's in thick with one of our witness/suspects. Too thick. I figure you're enough of a charmer you might just draw her off him. She's cute. Gorgeous even. Fair complexioned, like you, green eyes that could melt granite. Handsome lad meets lovely lady. And Tommy gets back to business, a sadder but wiser man."

"What happened to Gretchen?"

"Temporary setback in the romance."

"Your lovely lady a murderer?"

Joe shrugged. "I'll let you know." He realized Mel wasn't kidding. "I doubt it, for a couple reasons. She lost two years of her career when Corello croaked, and a lot of work. She would have been the only one to benefit from his reorganization plans. Yeah, she might be, but only if she's stupid."

"And all you want's hair samples?"

"Hair samples and to maintain good cooperative relationships with the people involved."

"Is this straight, Rodriguez?"

"Absolutely."

Mel stared at him long moments. He broke off the stare with another snort. "You either got enough brass to recast the Statue of Liberty, or you're nuts."

Joe was a sergeant. Mel was not. Technically, Joe could pull rank. Over and over, he asked the crew to downplay the rank. This was no time to bring it up. "Will you help me on this, Mel?"

He pressed his mouth into a thin line. "Maybe it's me who's nuts. Gimme your list."

Joe sent Mel off to Doug Hakamura with the names and got back to his paperwork, a reasonably happy man.

It was past 5 when he finally wrapped it. What next? Go home and see if Gretchen was surviving. Go see the kids. He'd spent only a couple hours with them since their return from Flag. He almost called the house to talk to Fel. Instead he found himself dialing the University.

Miss Watkins answered and announced she was about to go home. She transferred him to another secretary and a voice of unknown occupation. Finally he got through to Gary Collier. The man sounded younger on the phone than he looked in person.

"Good evening. Joe Rodriguez. I—"

"Hey, did you know some guy was around today to get some hair and fingernails? What's that all about?"

"Who was it?"

"Forget the name. Handsome sandy-haired guy; looks like he's into bodybuilding. Really mousy little lab assistant. I mighta seen the little guy before, but not the muscle man."

"Mel Carter and a tech named Hack."

"That's it. What were they looking for?"

"They probably would have said. Hey, I'm supposed to interrogate you some more. Want to go out for a bite?"

"My kind of third degree. Where?"

"I don't know the turf in Tempe. Recommend a place and I'll meet you there."

Collier did so. Twenty minutes later, Joe found himself in a crowded little place called Sipapu. It took him a moment to recall the meaning of the word; a sipapu was a hole in a ceremonial kiva, the entrance to the world of spirits.

Collier had arrived already. They bought a pitcher of said spirits and draped themselves across the bar making small talk for ten minutes until a booth opened up. Collier carried the glasses and Joe took the pitcher and potato chips. The bartender promised world-class hamburgers in ten minutes.

Joe scooted into the slick wood seat and refilled Collier's glass. "How come you didn't report the cobra and mamba missing—the snakes that ended up out in the compound?"

"Their cages were standing open. The cage doors were wide open. That means someone was using them. I mean someone qualified. One of our people."

"Using them how?"

Collier shrugged. He didn't seem to feel threatened by the questions, but that didn't mean a whole lot. "However. Take pictures. Milk them. Count scales for a paragraph you're writing on the taxonomy. Measure the penetration depth of the fangs. You name it. Two or three people were working on the cobra, for instance. It looked legit. I didn't think anything of it."

"Ruth Houser?"

"Yeah. And a kid in the Tri-Beta honors program—I think he's a junior—and Osada. He's trying to find links between Elapids and Colubrids."

"Who are they?"

"Cobra family and garter snake family."

"Assume everyone in the country is a suspect in the murder of Victor Corello. What would the motive be?"

Collier grunted. "The betterment of mankind. Doing the world a favor. Or at least the University. Anyone in the department would think, 'The department's better off without him. Deserving people will move up, the grad students who worked all those years will finally see fruit. Unless something's done, he's going to be there forever, constantly lousing things up. Making things really hard for everyone. He's all set and established–tenured, professional rep, in cozy with the top people–so he can dip around for years playing his games. But students and other profs have to get on with their lives, you know?' That's their motive."

"Suspect–perpetrator–whom would you tag?"

"Osada." Collier paused for a drink. "Phil's been held down a long time. He'd be out completely if Vic managed to pull off his reorganization."

"Lots of people can say that."

"There's more. You haven't known him long. Phil is extremely proud he's American. Makes a big thing of it. Follows hockey and basketball in the winter."

It took Joe a moment to catch on. "American sports not identified with the Japanese, such as baseball is, for instance."

"Exactly. He likes to think he's American as apple pie, but he's still very much old country. Traditional customs and attitudes."

"Like what?"

"Like saving face. You know how the Japanese are so concerned about saving face? Phil is, but he won't admit it. Vic humiliated him. In public. He made him lose face before his family, and you just don't do that with a Japanese, I don't care how American he thinks he is."

Joe digested this a while. "How about someone

not directly associated with the U? Corello's ex-wife, perhaps."

Collier pursed his lips in thought. He shook his head. "She lives out of state with two grown kids. Vic had next to no contact with them. No friction or flare-ups that I know of. In fact, she's remarried. No love, no hate, no animosity. Big zero."

"How would you rate Ruth as a suspect?"

"Bottom of the list. She loses the most if Corello dies. Top of the list for opportunity. She could do him a million ways, including the way that happened. And me. Don't leave me out. I'm a dandy suspect, because I had as many chances as Ruth and more motive. I hate his guts. Past tense. Hated."

"The department secretary, Sue Watkins?"

"She knows zip about snakes and venom and stuff. Strictly a good secretary, real efficient, but out to lunch otherwise. Besides, she might accidentally break a fingernail committing murder. Naa. Not her."

"Lowry?"

"Five on a scale of one to ten." Collier thought awhile. "No. Two at most. He's on the periphery. Kind of out of it around the department. Doesn't really know what's going on, or who does what. He wanders around in his own little world and doesn't care diddly-squat how the rest of the folks are spending their time and energy."

"Dorothy Stearns?"

"Grandmothers bake cookies and listen to your problems. They don't hang for murder."

"Gretchen said something about Mrs. Stearns

being a trusted confidante . . . that she knows all the couplings and gossip and such and keeps it to herself."

"Yeah. You can go to her with anything." Collier pondered the tabletop. Joe let the silence ride because Collier's mind seemed to be shifting gears. Such shifts were often productive in a casual conversation. "I did a little unloading on Grandma myself. Ruth and I were almost an item once, when I first arrived here. When it faded I needed someone to talk to."

"I didn't know that. Year ago, about?"

"Not quite. Closer to half a year."

"So what doused your love affair?"

Gary laughed. "Kinky. She's too kinky."

"Yeah, I guess any woman whose primary interest is snakes and lizards is a little weird. Ever since Eve, right?"

"Right. Not just that. Hey, I like snakes, and I'm not kinky. I mean sex." He leaned forward, elbows on the table. "She's all over you, leading you on. You get down to the basics and all of a sudden she pulls a switcheroo. Struggling to get away."

"Not sure I see what you mean."

"Like there's two women in her. One's a nympho to the max while you're messing around. You get all ready for the big time and the other hops out. A prude to the max. Hey, I couldn't take it. A couple times and I quit trying. Told her to go tease somebody else. Rotten shame too. I really like her. I think I could even love her, if it weren't for that."

"Marry her?"

"Maybe even that." Collier wagged his head. "But not like she is. Marriage has enough going against it without adding something like that."

"So you never consummated your love. When she fought, you backed off."

"No woman's worth a rape charge. Besides, when a woman panics like that at the last minute, you think maybe she has some sort of disease or something, and she got second thoughts, you know? Just in time. Yeah, I backed off."

They sat in silence awhile. Joe poured Collier another refill and nursed his own original glass along a little.

Collier talked more to the pitcher than to Joe, staring at the sweat beads on the fluted glass. "Her daddy's the real nut, you know. He's the one messed her head up with his lockstep religion. If it weren't for him, she'd probably be nice and normal."

"A nut. Big enough of a nut to kill somebody?"

Collier's eyes flicked up to Joe's, startled. He frowned. His eyes drifted back to the pitcher. "I never thought about it. You mean, kill the man he thinks took his daughter's virginity?"

"Something like that."

Collier shook his head. "Vic didn't. Take her virginity, I mean. Her daddy must've known she played around a lot before Vic. He was just the latest, is all."

"You said she cuts you off. Why not still a virgin?"

Collier's voice firmed up and took on almost a defensive edge. "I like to think I'm a rational person. Mind over matter, right?"

"Scientific outlook."

"Exactly. I'm as macho as the next guy, but I also like to think my brain's in control. She calls it off, I have the will to stop. Mind over matter. But she must've teased along some hurking, brain-dead football player—more than one, I bet—who wasn't going to stop just 'cause the whistle blew. She couldn't lead some guys on as far as she does and expect them not to . . . " He shook his head. "She lost it long ago. And Vic had her for sure."

"Would her father suspect a love match between her and Vic?"

"He claims she's a virgin, but I'm not so sure he believes it. But it's hard to tell with him. He's so bombastic."

"But you're confident something was on between them."

Collier leaned forward again and dropped his voice to a near murmur. "Vic got her pregnant a couple months ago. Little Miss Daughter of the High and Mighty Religious Man had an abortion."

A Little Slack

Well, speaking frankly, Corello was a donkey, but he was a brilliant donkey."

Joe watched this department chairman—make that chairperson—with his effusive doublespeak, and he pictured his own division captain. They were cut from the same bolt, these two. They even looked a little alike: a bit flabby from too much desk work, a bit pallid from too much indoor sunshine, more than a bit bombastic. Same gray suits.

The chairman continued. "He brought a great deal of favorable publicity to the University and to our Life Sciences department. VARI is world renowned. So we cut him a little slack."

"A little? It seems you cut him as much as he wanted."

"He put the department on the map."

Joe relaxed back in his chair and paused a moment, thinking how to frame this next question for maximum irritation. "You've been evading conversation with me for days, ever since I threatened you with arrest if you stepped out into the enclosure at the Life Sciences building."

"Nonsense. I'd forgotten all about that."

"Department heads never forget being challenged on their own turf, ordered around. But now I'm wondering to myself if your evasion might not be more than that. Might you not be directly involved in Vincent Corello's death?"

"That's actionable, detective. Unless you have proof—and I'm certain there is none—I can have your—"

Joe raised his voice enough to cut him off. "Your Dr. Corello was more than an embarrassment inside the department. He was a liability. Everything he touched was going down the tubes—morale, productivity, reputation—"

The fellow blustered loudly.

Joe pressed on above the protests. "He was going great guns as a popular guru, a public figure. But professionally, he was losing it, and professional competence is how a university is measured. He had grad students working on pointless projects, projects neither they nor other professors could make head or tail of."

"That's not so. He—"

"There was no easy way to simply fire him since he was tenured. You could not risk adverse publicity, and adverse publicity was bound to crop up sooner or later when the department blew sky-high. So you contracted out his demise, removing him in a manner that would put the department in the public eye; not with the revelation of professional embarrassment but with a tragedy. Public and professional sympathy accrues instead of ridicule. And he's safely in the grave before his errors become obvious."

Were scowls microwaves, Joe would have cooked in ten seconds flat. The chairman was so mad his voice squeaked a bit. "Am I to believe this is your notion of competent investigation?"

"It's a valid hypothesis, framed from compelling circumstantial evidence." Joe kept his face and hands relaxed. He waited. How much did this man know about what really went on in the department? He watched. As moments ticked by the answer became obvious: not a thing.

"What compelling evidence?"

"Detailed in the supplemental reports to my lieutenant. In summary, derived from both deliberate and unintentional remarks by those under Corello. And beside him. Of professional incompetence, racism, chauvinism, moral turpitude, rule by divine fiat subject to whim."

"He had enemies. You can't believe everything they say."

"He had no friends. I weighed that. But when I assemble all the testimony of numerous people associated formally and informally with him, this picture emerges. I cannot disregard it."

The man's scowl had mellowed out to an intense stare. "I believe from here on, you should talk only to my lawyer."

"As you wish." Joe sat forward as if to prepare to

rise. "I can assume too that we'll need a court order for your department records?"

"What records?"

"Corello's file, for starters. Surely the young black man, Jim Craig, filed a complaint when Corello called him 'Jim Crow' to his face. And Dr. Osada has been the subject of racial harassment on numerous occasions. I'm therefore assuming—"

"I never heard of such a thing! Is that what Craig told you?"

"No. He was already dying when we first spoke. Other sources. I'm therefore assuming that all that went into Corello's file. Of course, if it's not all present in his file, with such overwhelming evidence for the existence of these complaints, we would have to assume Corello's file was altered, either before or after his death. Someone protecting him or protecting the department."

"What do you want, detective?"

"Corello's murderer."

"I mean, what do you want from me? There aren't any complaints of that sort. Nothing like that ever came to me. Why are you doing this?"

"You're telling me the head of the department hasn't a clue as to what was happening on his own turf? I can't believe that." Joe wagged his head. "You're not a fool."

"That's the first straight thing you've said today. No, I'm not a fool. If anything like that had crossed my desk I would have investigated. There were no complaints."

"And Osada never approached you privately about Corello's bigotry against Japanese?"

"Never."

"Or Craig."

"Never."

"And no woman ever complained about being unable to complete a doctorate under him? Intriguing." Joe stood up. "I'll send some folks around this afternoon with the court order. Thank you for your time, sir."

He walked out of the office on thick shag carpet, into a reception area far more graciously decorated than the austere, bare walls of the Life Sciences building. The secretary smiled at him as he left. Already her telephone was lighting up.

Tommy, one of the few people who can sprawl while standing up, lurched erect from his angle of repose against the wall. "How'd it go?"

"Got him nervous as a long-tailed cat in a room full of rockers. I still don't see the advantage here."

"Sit back and see what he stirs up." Tommy started off down the hall toward the outside doors. "He can reach into corners we know nothing about. Watch and wait. Just a hunch on me own part."

"Actually, I kind of like the idea that the chairman was in on the kill. Who besides Corello was chummy with him?"

"No one, that meself has noticed, as, for instance, in comments and asides. Would not have to be chummy; the department head can order about anyone he cares to, and probably would not lay such a task upon a chum."

"True." Joe flipped open his appointment book. The chairman's name was the last on the page. "My place for dinner and paperwork? Jerry's really getting on my case about turning in the supplementals. He wants to know what's happening, he says." Joe pushed out into the heat. "I guess the Tempe commander keeps calling him up."

That got Tom started on how the upper echelons don't care about getting the job done, but rather about looking good in the eyes of other upper echelon people. Joe wouldn't put Jerry in that category, really, but he didn't argue. The monologue lasted all the way from the University to Joe's apartment.

Tommy pulled his bug into a guest parking slot. They trooped up the stairs to the second-floor landing. The door swung open before Joe could stick his key in the lock. Cool air whooshed out. Joe and Tommy whooshed in. Tommy headed right off to the bathroom.

Gretchen closed the door. "Saw you coming. You're early."

"Paperwork. You're looking a lot better. Good color. Twinkle's back." Joe flopped down at the table and shoved his briefcase aside for the moment. Sufficient unto the day . . .

"Feel a million times better. Might even survive." Gretchen grinned charmingly and sat down across from him, rejoining her tall glass of ginger ale.

Joe looked around. He recognized the faint dust smell of the vacuum cleaner hanging on the air. "You cleaned the joint up. Vacuum, dust, the whole works."

"Just a little thank-you. And I repeat my thanks. What you did was pure friendship love." Then Gretchen's demeanor chilled. Joe knew without looking that Tommy was entering the dining alcove.

"Gretch." Tommy pulled his jacket off, unhooked his tie, fiddled with shirt buttons as he sat down. "Thought you'd be home by now."

"I'm well enough. I just wanted to say, thank you before I left. Besides, I'm feeling confrontational."

"Confrontational? Eh, the luck of the Irish be with me today!"

Joe stood up and went into the kitchen. He was eight feet away from them, their meeting hardly private, but it seemed better somehow that he not be sitting there. He took off his own jacket and tie and dug into the fridge for a beer for Tommy and into the cupboard for a cola for himself.

"I talked to Doug this afternoon on the phone." Apparently Gretchen wasn't getting confrontational yet. "He's done with the hair. The only one to show slight arsenic contamination is Dorothy Stearns. Also, she bleaches and colors her hair."

Joe suggested, "Probably salt and pepper in real life."

"No doubt." Gretchen took another sip of ginger ale. "So it looks like Granny was trying to poison the dork."

"Who would think it!" Tom purred. "Sweet little old lady like that. So sincere."

"Sincerely homicidal." Gretchen wagged her head. "Maybe. It could also be circumstantial. She's in the coffee room. Arsenic was in the coffee room. She picked it up accidentally."

"Good enough to get an indictment?" Joe popped the beer and took it out to Tom.

"Probably not. It's contamination for sure, but the source is iffy. Hack says he thinks they got samples from everybody who could possibly have access to the coffee room. No students. Faculty lounge. All doctoral students and staff."

"And volunteers." Joe leaned in the archway between kitchen and alcove.

"And volunteers."

"Trespassing students," Tom ventured.

Joe nodded. "Something we'll have to bring up casually; ask people offhandedly if they happened to notice anyone other than faculty. It would have to be someone making multiple visits. They'll mention Jason Houser, for example."

"Who came up clean. Mel got samples from him too." Gretchen stared off across the room. "So that makes you guys bad guys, you know, prosecuting Granny. Nobody took *Psycho* seriously. Granny can't do murder. Besides, in *Psycho,* it turned out that it wasn't Granny after all. Even Hitchcock can't make Granny into a murderer."

"You saying we should cut Dorothy Stearns some slack?" Joe asked. "Not at least confront her about attempted murder because she's over sixty-five?"

Gretchen shrugged.

Joe stared at the top of his cola can and thought about Dorothy Stearns a little. But mostly he thought about how utterly stupid it is to buy a nutritionally worthless soft drink in an aluminum can, drink the contents, and throw the can away. And how slow the Phoenix ruling fathers are about getting any kind of sound recycling program rolling. And how his ancestors sipped water directly from springs and seeps and were all the better off for it. Progress.

"Look," Gretchen pressed on. " 'The rest of your natural life' means one thing to us, and something altogether different to her. She doesn't have all that much of her natural life left. So you haul her before a judge. So she gets convicted. Even admits it, probably. She's honest to a fault. What have you done?"

Tom shook his head. "Your defense be eloquent but hardly necessary. Meself cannot picture Jerry preferring charges on such flimsy evidence. He'll cut her the slack, as ye call it."

Gretchen turned on him, exploding, her eyes ablaze. "And what would you know about cutting any slack?"

"Methinks I smell confrontation anear."

"And don't try to make it sound cute—dismiss what I'm saying with some glib little remark. You do that a lot. I have never slept with Joe, and as far as I know I never will. But he befriended me, freely and generously. Cleaning up after someone with gut-rot is as free and generous as you can get. He exercised friendship, Tommy. *Friendship.* And it wasn't sexual. It doesn't have to be sexual. I asked you to back off for pers—"

" 'Tis one thing to develop platonic friendships, Gretch. 'Tis quite another to take a lover and then summarily dismiss the relationship."

"Your attitude is that I'm pursuing some whim. Well, what you see as a whim, Tom, I see as a crisis of conscience. You blew up and said you cared about me, but that I didn't care anything about your feelings. A week later you're in someone else's arms. Who's giving who the raw deal here?"

"You're making assumptions that—"

"Wasn't I worth waiting for while I resolve this?"

Joe backed away quietly and busied himself building tossed salads. Two salads. He'd be feeding Tom here tonight, or Gretchen. But not both of them.

Tom, for once, seemed to be without words.

Gretchen still had torrents of them. "You'd mumble in my ear how much you cared about me. But when I needed some space you didn't care enough to cut me a little slack. Not any at all." She took a deep breath and the tears poured forth, but she didn't snuffle or sob.

Joe would be feeding Gretchen. Tom bolted to his feet and gathered up his jacket and briefcase. "I've work to do aplenty, and I'll not get much done here." He glanced at Joe. "We've a squad meeting on the morrow, 8 A.M. I'll meet ye at the shop at quarter till to compare notes." He let himself out the door.

Gretchen dissolved then, and Joe let her weep and wail in peace. For one thing, he had no idea what to say. He started the chicken cooking and put a couple potatoes on.

And he thought about Ruth Houser. Tommy was fickle. He was, in many ways, amoral. But Joe had never known him to hop from bed to bed quite so swiftly. What were the particular charms of Miss Houser that he would so easily put Gretchen aside—on the surface, if not in his heart?

What keys did Ruth Houser hold that Joe needed to unlock this mystery?

Chickens Home to Roost

Joe sat stretched across the kitchen counter, his shoulders against the cupboard and his bare feet hanging out over the sink. He idly studied his ankles, one bulbous and the other lean and angular, as Marie described her terrible, horrible, miserable day at work. Her voice paused.

He picked it up. "So here you are up past 11 at night, your time, talking on the phone, when you ought to be sleeping."

"Isn't it stupid, what you do for love?" She giggled. "How are Gretchen and Tommy doing?"

"Impasse, same as before."

"Poor Gretchen. I know what she's going through. It's so hard to know where the line is. I don't mean faith in Jesus—that's clearly defined—but . . . let's see, how do I say this? Deciding where to walk the line between casual and strict. Exactly what's moral and proper. 'Moral' and 'proper' are different, you know. You have a whole spectrum within the faith."

A thought struck him. "Gretchen grew up with no religious training at all. How about if you grew up under very demanding and narrow fundamentalism? Is it easier to buy into a strict morality or harder?"

She giggled again. "First you join Fundamentalists Anonymous. Then you join a liberal church. Then you quit both. Then you pray and say, 'God, now I'm totally confused.' "

"Fundamentalists Anonymous? Right. And the parallel group is Fund-Anon, and the kids go to Funda-Teen, and . . . "

"No, really, Joe, there actually is one. People who are trying to shake the narrow, legalistic mind-set they grew up with."

"Really. How do I find it?"

"Look in the phone book. Or the library. Or call up the local AA chapter and ask them. They'll know if there's one around." Her voice paused. "I thought you grew up nominal Catholic."

"Just curious about what I'm missing." *Thinking about Ruth and Jason Houser.*

The next day he searched the phone book in vain and ended up calling the library hot line. They gave him a name and number. That same night he found himself sitting on a steel folding chair in a featureless room furnished only with other steel folding chairs. They were arranged in a circle, King Arthur's Knights of the Round Table without a table. Seven people besides Joe arrived and settled themselves into the cruel chairs. Somebody's drip coffee machine, more or less the focus of attention, sputtered in the middle of the circle. A stack of styro cups lay beside it, but all seven of these anonymous fundamentalists had brought their own ceramic mugs.

The facilitator, a youngish man with a neatly trimmed dark beard, followed the classic Alcoholics Anonymous format of such meetings worldwide. He introduced himself as Ed, using the AA precept of first names only.

Joe, the only stranger present, cleared his throat. "My name is Joe, and you may not want me here. I trust that if you prefer I leave, you'll say so. I'm not a fundamentalist—never was—and that's why I came. I'm a police officer investigating a crime in which fundamentalists are closely involved. I know nothing about them—how their minds operate, what their reactions to a given situation would be—nothing. I'm trying to get a behavioral perspective on these people."

Ed's cheek twitched, jiggling his beard a bit. "They're accused of a crime? Violent or white-collar?"

"Violent crime. Not accused, at least, not so far. Involved. To what degree, I don't know."

An overweight girl in her mid-twenties laughed. "I'm speaking only for myself here, but this seems like an interesting way to see myself a little better. I'd like to help you out, Joe, because there's so much misunderstanding. I admire the way you're approaching it. And I think your questions, the questions of an outsider, might raise some issues that we on the inside don't talk about, or are in denial about."

"Good point!" An older woman chimed in. "Joe, you might give us fodder for weeks of discussion."

Ed looked from face to face. "We have two positive responses. Does anyone have a negative feeling?"

No comments.

"Tell you what, Joe. If for some reason any of us become uncomfortable about your presence, now or later, we'll mention it and you'll leave. Is that agreeable?"

"More than agreeable. I'm grateful."

When Ed smiled, his whole beard rearranged itself. "Good. Joe, the reason we might start feeling uncomfortable is that we really open up in here. Let it all fly. No pretense. Well, that's not *exactly* true. Pretense was a big part of our lives for a long time. We still tend to slip into it, but much reduced pretense."

All six chuckled knowingly.

"Go ahead. Ask us something," the heavy girl urged him.

"Very well." Joe tried to get comfortable on this chair. Fat chance. He tipped it back to two legs—a risky thing to do with a folding chair—and laced his fingers behind his head. "Let's say the people I want to know more about are one person, and we'll call him "Fundy." I assume Fundy has been working hard his whole life to get into heaven. Were he to break a commandment, would he doom himself to hell? Or might he have a way out?"

Ed looked around the circle. "Pete, you can address that."

Pete, short and rotund, could stand to lose fifty pounds. Was excessive weight a characteristic of all fundamentalists with problems, and if so, did that mean the svelte Ruth Houser was dealing successfully with any she might have?

Pete dropped forward, his elbows on his knees. "In that regard, Joe, Fundy is one of two stripes. Noncharismatic fundies, such as some kinds of Baptists, usually believe in 'once saved always saved.' Once Christ claims you—"

"And that's Jesus Christ's decision, not yours," the older lady butted in.

Pete never lost stride. "Right. Once God claims you, God won't let you go. Chasten you, yes, but you're guaranteed a place in heaven no matter what. The other stripe, most of them the charismatics such as the AG's . . . "

"Who?"

"Assemblies of God. They believe you can lose your salvation by turning away from God."

"But not from an accidental misstep?"

"Maybe. Depends on the group."

"Which stripe does Scripture support?"

"Either, depending on how you interpret certain passages. Despite the scriptural ambiguity, you can be sure your Fundy will be adamantly on one side of the fence or the other."

Joe made a mental note to engage Houser in a discussion about salvation. "Either stripe, he relies utterly on the inerrant and literal Scripture?"

"That's the idea."

That older woman kicked in again. "The trouble comes when your Fundy relies on his personal interpretation—not what the words say, but what he claims they mean—and that's a big difference. There's a lot of that especially in certain independent churches. Churches outside denominations. They even give their own meanings to the words and then claim that that's what God means too."

"Salvation?"

The facilitator wagged his head. "No ambiguity there. Jesus Christ died to save sinners. You accept that fact, release your life to Him, and He becomes your eternal salvation. We're Christians, Joe. Hurting and trying to heal, but safe in Christ."

"Some of us," the overweight girl corrected. "I used to be. I'm so sour on Jesus Christ now, I don't know what I am."

Joe nodded thoughtfully. "To an outsider, Fundy is excessively concerned with outward appearance. Is this anywhere near an accurate observation?"

"Right on!" The heavy girl launched a discussion that became ten minutes of war stories from most of the people here. She told of being punished for shaving her legs when she was twelve. She told about the strictures of dress and hairstyle, the proscription of makeup. She said she never questioned the oft-quoted maxim that the outside reveals the inside; that if you hold to the proper beliefs, your appearance must reflect that. She mentioned its opposite, that if the outside looks good, the inside must be good also.

The older woman talked about arbitrary rules of behavior, and Joe perceived as she spoke that her husband had left her for a younger woman. Pete told about people denied fellowship and dissuaded from attending a certain church because their hair was too long, their hemlines too short, their faces unshaven.

Ed had claimed they let it all fly here. Joe looked right at him. "So your beard there is a form of rebellion?"

"Absolutely. You bet. To this day my father refuses to speak to me until I shave. I'm thirty-three years old, but I'm not supposed to make that decision for myself."

"And you'll notice," the older woman jumped in again, "it's not a decision about theology or faith. A hundred years ago it wouldn't have mattered a bit, because beards were common then. The biggest men in the faith wore them. Moody, Hudson Taylor, you name it. Jesus probably had a beard. David did for sure. And yet now, a clean face is right up there next to Jesus Himself."

Joe frowned. He was hoping to get an objective viewpoint on Ruth and Jason Houser's religion here. Instead, he was being drowned in bitterness. It came through in their words, in their tone of voice, in their gestures of helplessness. These people seemed to have nothing positive to give each other. He wasn't certain they had anything positive to give him. "So we're talking about cultural standards here, not faith as such. Is it a generational thing within the fundamentalist groups themselves? I mean, are the arbitrary standards of appearance changing as the old guard dies off? How can I say this? Can Fundy's son have a different attitude from Fundy about what constitutes the correct appearance and still embrace the faith as tightly as Fundy does?"

"To an extent. Change doesn't come fast, though."

"Let's say Fundy's son is a daughter. Uh, make-up, skirts slightly above the knee, stylish blouses, possibly even provocative, but not excessively so. How would you interpret her dress? Or a teen son in tight jeans and quarterback hairstyle."

"That's a loaded question. I hope you have an hour to spare." An older man in expensive slacks and a polo shirt spoke for the first time. "Two things come into play here with your hypothetical girl, her own struggles and her mother's. She's rebelling against the bonds she grew up in. Chances are excellent her mother is sexually repressed and probably dominated by a strongly authoritarian husband. Her mother has no life of her own, and no latitude to make decisions; lots of unfulfilled . . . uh . . . " He glanced toward the older woman.

" . . . yearnings." The woman responded instantly. "Needs. She needs to be a whole person and can't."

"And her daughter picks up that unfinished business and plays it out. She is living her mother's life vicariously. What I mean is, she's rebelling and making decisions, all the things her mother would like to do but won't."

"You're saying she's acting out the rebellion her mother cannot express for one reason or another."

"That's right. And the mother is probably sending mixed messages about it. On the outside she supports her husband's oppressive attitudes. She preaches to the daughter or the son following her husband's line. But her unspoken feelings—"

"Suppressed. Subliminal?"

The man nodded vigorously. "Precisely. The subliminal, unconscious message she sends the daughter is 'Go for it! Do what I don't have the guts to do.' "

" 'Give your father the hard time I wish I could give him.' "

"You got it. And, it can be cross-gender. Sons can act out mothers' unfulfilled needs, daughters can act out fathers'. Also, a person can be deeply angry at someone and transfer that anger, take it out on someone else."

Joe chuckled. "I do that every day. Bad day at work, I yell at the kids. And a traffic cop pulls some doofus over for speeding. He either gives him a ticket or unloads on him, but not both. He can dump three or four bad days on the poor guy—rain all over him—and he'll smile and say thank you."

All seven laughed.

The well-dressed man nodded. "We all do that. But you realize what you're doing. Your traffic cop is venting his anger deliberately. Rebellion and anger that are not consciously acknowledged can be transferred without realizing it. You hate your mother, but society doesn't allow you to hate your mother, so you say hateful things to your wife or sister or teacher or friend."

"And it takes a counselor to figure out what's happening?"

"Some pretty deep analysis, and that's another thing Fundy won't sit still for. Counseling and analysis. Any word starting with *psycho-* turns him off.

And yet, unless the inner drives are uncovered, the whole family suffers."

"And none of them knows why they're hurting."

"That's it. Basically you have a kid rebelling and doing things that Fundy hates, or thinks is sinful, or that the kid hopes will shock Fundy. If you ask the kid why he's doing them, he or she will answer, 'I don't know.' And the kid's answer will be truthful. He really doesn't know. He's acting out the family pain and he doesn't consciously know he's doing it."

"Driven by circumstances he doesn't know about. To what degree? How far will he go? He or she?"

The nattily attired man shrugged. "I'm a counselor. Social services. I had a kid in counseling a couple years ago. She was eight years old." His voice caught. "She set her brother on fire. Another, a boy of thirteen, walked up to a kid he disliked at school and stuck a knife in him. No apparent provocation. Both kids came from very strict, religious families."

"I worked on that boy's case," Joe said. "The prosecutor attempted to try him as an adult but the judge wouldn't buy it. Still pending."

"Most cases, and there are thousands and thousands of them, are not dramatic like that. Most are very subtle."

"A lot of the problems in legalistic families could be ironed out with counseling." The heavy girl leaned forward earnestly. "But most of those families are run by an authoritative male who doesn't think there's a problem. Especially because so often he *is* the problem. And unless he thinks there's a problem, no one gets help. So you never hear about all the pain and struggle."

Joe sat forward too. His chair creaked. "What we're talking about here isn't religion. It's control issues."

"That's right!" The girl bobbed her head triumphantly. "And too often, it's wrapped in religion. 'Jesus wouldn't want you doing this. God will get you if you do that.' There's a name for it. Spiritual abuse."

Was that what Joe saw in the Houser household? Spiritual abuse? And if so, was it pertinent to his investigation? "How do I know the difference? I haven't been into religion very long."

Ed thought about that a moment. "Jesus. Listen to what the person says about Jesus and how he says it. He or she. Is Jesus a club to keep people under control, or does that person really, genuinely hold Jesus in affection? It's not foolproof, but it's a good indication. Jesus isn't supposed to be the author of pain and struggle . . . not the kind we've been going through."

"Now I'm really going to reverse my welcome by being unpardonably rude." Joe looked straight at the heavy girl. "You're grossly overweight. Is that tied to the pain and struggle you're all talking about?"

And she never batted an eye. "Yes, I am," she replied evenly. "Grossly. You're right. You see, my response was food-oriented. I dealt with the pain I couldn't deal with any other way by eating. My father could control my friends, my life, and make all my decisions, but he couldn't control my eating. I could always sneak food. I weigh forty-two pounds less than I did a year ago. It's going to take me a long time. I still have a powerful urge to eat whenever something goes wrong."

"Forty-two pounds." Joe wagged his head. "My sincerest compliments! That's wonderful. All right, yours was food. Ed's here is a beard. Food, though, might not be a problem for someone else, right?"

"Right."

"So does something else have to be? If a person is under an unyielding authority, is he or she absolutely going to kick over the traces one way or another?"

Ed opened that one up to general discussion. Another half hour of war stories went by in which Joe learned nothing new, as such, except the verity that people are going let off steam. He kept comparing these admissions to what he knew of Ruth Houser's life.

Finally he asked, "You're all talking about uncontrollable behavior. If a person is assuming the outward appearance of a rebel, is that enough? I mean, will the mere appearance of rebellion suffice, or must there be a behavioral aspect to that rebellion as well?"

They failed to agree on that. Some said there is almost certainly an uncontrollable behavioral aspect as well. Others said looking the part of a rebel is enough. Finally the topic cooled off.

Joe was going to jump into the lull with another question, but Ed spoke. "The phenomenon called 'splitting off' applies here. The most blatant example I can think of is a preacher who hired a prostitute to display herself and titillate him in a motel room."

"What hurt most," the interruptive lady added, "was that it wasn't plain old sexual immorality. It was kinky. Immoral sex is a no-no, but weirdness is a super no-no. If he simply had sex with her, it wouldn't have seemed as bad in the eyes of people to whom appearance is everything—" She wagged her head.

"Good point." Ed chuckled. "Anyway, this guy had just written about sexual purity. Very rigid, turn-of-the-century approach. He didn't even like mixed bathing at the public pool. The press had a feeding frenzy. 'How can a guy say something like that in a book and then turn around and do that stuff in a motel room?' They couldn't grasp the answer."

"And the answer is. . . ?" Joe took the cue.

"Glad you asked. The fundamentalist is not a hypocrite in the usual sense of the word. We've been talking a lot about how important appearance is, pretense, even. But Fundy is absolutely sincere about it. He's making the best appearance he can for the best of reasons. He wants Jesus to look good, and if Fundy looks good, he doesn't make Jesus look bad. That's extremely important to him. Present a good clean picture of the church for the world to see. Don't let the warts show."

"Just the same as an officer in uniform is supposed to keep his shoes polished. Good reflection on the department. Including the preacher you just mentioned?"

"I don't doubt his sincerity for a moment. And the military, the same thing. Exactly. Part of the Christian's uniform is his halo, and you gotta keep it polished, so the world will see only the best part of the faith. And good behavior indicates a good attitude. If I dot all my i's and cross all my t's, every one of them, that indicates to some people that I'm saved."

Joe pursed his lips a moment. "A tree is known by its fruit."

The older woman interrupted again. "The tree has no power to change the kind of fruit it puts out. It's automatic. And a human being doesn't much listen to his head. I read where 80 percent or more of our so-called conscious decisions are actually made subconsciously, beyond reach of reason. My husband, for instance. Two years ago he refused to associate with a couple after they divorced. Another time he blocked the ordination of a pastor whose wife had left him. Said divorce was sin. Then he met another woman and didn't want to be married to me anymore. Suddenly divorce is all right under certain circumstances. You see? His heart made this decision that went against everything his head said, and his head did the flipflop. Heart makes the choices. Not head."

"Does the head know what's going on?"

"Probably not." The overweight girl sat forward. "An authoritative male may claim, 'This is what Scripture says,' and that may not be what Scripture says at all. It's his heart talking. But he's sure his head is doing the interpreting."

"He might commit sin and say it's right instead of wrong? How far astray can he go without realizing it?"

"A long, long way. You talked about violent

crime. He could commit a violent crime and claim it's what God wanted, or that it was to protect the name of Jesus, or whatever. I'm thinking now of the man accused of shooting an abortionist."

Joe looked from face to face. These people seemed eager to help. "So he rationalizes. Immorality becomes morality. If a crime is committed, who will commit it, a man or a woman?"

"The man." Three voices said it simultaneously. The divorced woman's voice prevailed. "Usually. He is *usually* the actor. Women are reactors. He is the head of the house. She is programmed to yield. He initiates. She rarely does."

"So if he goes astray, it's because he's leading himself astray?"

The man in the suit spoke again. "That's what I meant by splitting off. I'm sure that preacher truly believes what he wrote about the sin of sex. And I'm convinced he did not want to behave immorally. But he was denying a lot of himself—denying that he's a sexual being with strong physical needs. He refused to admit that you can't just turn off sexuality, or any other natural, God-given part of yourself, because you think it's dirty or could lead to sin. He split it off by denying its existence and its power over him, and so it took on a life of its own. When something is split off, it might take some other form. It might even get picked up by the kids."

"He was driven to what he did?"

"Just like the kids who take over the parents' unfinished business and then can't understand why they do what they do. He refused to deal with his sexual identity, splitting it off, you see; so his sexual identity manifested itself in unwholesome ways beyond his control."

"So where is good old personal responsibility and self-control in all this?"

"Fundy exercises it a lot more than you'd guess. He's extremely serious about personal responsibility. And control—he shows incredible control. He keeps such a tight lid on things that when something blows, it blows all to hades."

Joe nodded. "Like a head of steam—don't let any out and too much pressure builds."

"That's it. I'm not excusing or condoning rebellion or sin. I believe a person is held responsible for his action. His or hers. I'm just telling you how it happens to some people. Sneaks up on them."

"I see. Is only the sexual identity vulnerable to being split off?"

The voice of the well-dressed man was probably radio-trained. It purred along without stumbling, every word precise. "Any aspect of the human personality. And, it might express itself in some other way altogether. For example, the sexual aspect need not manifest itself sexually."

"That was going to be my next question, but I didn't know how to frame it." Joe pondered the matter a few moments. "So then, if a person buries a problem or drive or aspect of his personality, that problem will dig itself up somehow. But the disinterment need not be in the same context as the problem." He frowned at his confusing, convoluted thought.

"Exactly! Disinterment . . . good word for it." The man in the suit grinned. The grin faded. "These legalistic Christians claim Jesus cures them of lust or greed or alcoholism or ingrown toenails. In some cases, I suppose Jesus does. But in the vast majority, those human needs and faults and problems aren't really cured. They're split off."

"You can shoo the chickens away, but rest assured, they'll come home to roost."

And all seven heads were nodding.

BURDENS

People who are genetically prone to putting on weight can look at a picture of celery and get fat eyeballs. Others can tank up on 5,000 calories a day and stay slim enough to slip through fence pickets. Doug Hakamura was somewhere in between. At lunchtime, he opened up his Eskimo cooler and at the end of lunch he closed it. In between the opening and the closing, he ate, delicately, methodically, constantly. He wasn't exactly fat from all this intake, but his proportions were somewhat wider than most.

Today Doug sat across from Joe in the lab lunchroom, surrounded by wrappers, sandwich bags, and little Tupperware containers. "Want some more chips and dip?"

Joe raised a hand. "No thanks. 'Preciate your sharing your lunch with me." Under normal circumstances he would feel a little guilty about letting a man share half his lunch with him, but Doug Hakamura's lunch was not normal.

Doug grinned. "Gretchen and Hack call my lunch box 'the cornucopia.' " He leaned back and scooped up a pile of file folders at the far end of the table. "Here's your latest. Official revelation on the arsenic contamination angle, and all the other stuff." He handed Joe another day of reading. "Did you talk to Tommy about that coroner who did the report on the snakebite victim eighteen months ago?"

"Yeah. Real botch job. They didn't even save the snake. No sign of a bite, entry point of the venom not established, culpability of the snake not established. Tommy says the guy who signed it, since retired, is scared spitless of snakes."

"Sheesh." Doug wagged his head. "Wish I could just ignore anything I'm scared of. I'd quit working on AIDS stuff."

Joe leafed through the report in which he had the greatest vested interest, the field station site. He grunted. "Osada fingerprints? What was Osada doing out there?"

"Prints didn't say, and we can't be sure he was there. We found what we think are Osada prints, on a funny box out in the storage shed and also on one of the snake sticks propped against the wall. Inconclusive."

"Funny box . . . varnished wood with a sliding lid?"

"Yeah. What do they use them for?"

"Transporting snakes and stuff. What about the

tire tracks in the wash? Did you—here they are." Joe pulled the sheets out and folded them up.

"Rodriguez, you poop. I put this beautiful report together and you tear it apart."

"Just borrowing the tracks. Gonna try to find a match."

"Run every tire in Tempe through a mud hole?"

"A few driveways might do it." Joe glanced at his watch. "Thanks again for the lunch. Also the sports rundown. I always like to know the inside scoop on why my teams are losing."

"Pick better teams, Joe." Doug started scooping up lunch debris, the wrappers in one pile, the Tupperware and edible leftovers back into his lunch box.

Joe left the room and stood in the entryway by the double doors awhile and thought. Things were starting to fall together somewhat, a lot of small questions clearing, but the big question remained elusive. Who actually killed Vic Corello? He walked outside and around the building to his MG.

Twenty years ago, Phoenix in midsummer was a ghost town. The snowbirds would come flying down from the north in October and depart around Easter. Throughout the long hot spring, summer, and early fall, milk would drop to 29 cents a half gallon because the cows kept producing and the milk drinkers had all gone home to cooler climes. You could drive from light to light without getting behind another car. You and a salesclerk might be the only persons in a big dime store or pharmacy.

Not these days. Phoenix was a genuine year-round city now, with permanent industry, permanent residents, and permanent law enforcement problems. Joe drove through traffic that was not much lighter than in November, out across the Van Buren/Mill Avenue bridge to Tempe.

Philip Osada lived south of the U in one of the old, genteel, upper-bracket neighborhoods that were fast disappearing in Tempe. Joe matched a well-landscaped Spanish style bungalow against the address in his notebook, but he could have told you without the match this was Osada's home. A big, dusty, mud-caked Toyota four-by sat in the driveway. Osada did a lot of fieldwork. This was a field-worker's vehicle.

Joe rang the doorbell and waited, rang again and waited. Inside the house, a tiny silky terrier hopped up on a sofa back and barked out the window at him. No one chased the pooch off the furniture. No one answered the door.

Joe walked over to the four-by and gave the cab a cursory once-over. The back was cluttered with buckets, wire cages, burlap bags, ropes, loose camping gear, a couple of lanterns, and some of those snake boxes. Then he knelt down by the back wheels, his tire prints in hand, to answer the question that brought him here. Could Osada's vehicle have gone out to the field station?

It could. He headed back to the University.

When Osada dismissed his afternoon session in the big lecture hall in Life Sciences, Joe was waiting for him at the door.

Dr. Osada smiled graciously. "Good to see you again. What can I do for you?"

"Give me half an hour of your valuable time—a

big favor to ask."

"But not an unreasonable one, considering the circumstances." He turned to a man in his thirties hovering nearby. "Mr. Hayes, I really should attend to this gentleman first. I'm sorry. Can we discuss your concerns in an hour or so, say, around 4?"

"Sure." The man put a smiling face on his disappointment. "Your office?"

"Yes. Thank you."

Joe smiled too. "I appreciate this, Mr. Hayes. Thank you." He fell in beside Dr. Osada, headed for the elevator. "Your class looks older than I would expect."

"Nearly all public school teachers working on their masters'." Osada hit the up button. He wagged his head. "Some of the horror tales they tell!"

"Of life in the trenches?"

"I decry the lack of academic interest in today's students. And yet, actually, I have it easy."

The doors wheezed open. Joe stepped inside and let Osada recount secondhand war stories from high school teachers as they walked to his office. When they entered the office Joe closed the outer door. The move was not lost on Dr. Osada. The gentleman brought his own chair around to the open aisle so that the desk would raise no barrier, and waved a hand for Joe to sit down.

Dr. Osada cleared a chair off for himself and settled into it. "We were going to get together to discuss the Indians' attitudes and approach to snakes, but I trust that's not what this meeting is about. What do we have, detective?"

"A theory, doctor." Joe sat back and propped the tips of his fingers together into an A. "Shamed and frustrated by the director's capricious behavior, you decided something must be done. You have no influence—no clout, as it's called. Yet, so long as Dr. Corello remains in his position, there is no real chance of improvement for your situation, or for that of any of the colleagues and graduate students you know and admire. And his proposed restructuring would destroy your world and that of many others.

"You set a devious trap for Corello, a trap that can never be laid at your door. You know he often sneaks around out at his field station, checking up on his students. You know he has a severe heart condition. So you clip the fangs of a rattler, a *Crotalus mitchelli* to be precise, and take it out to the station in a varnished wooden box. In all this you are doing nothing untoward as regards appearance. You are a student of snakes; you're expected to haul them around.

"You find the perfect place to put that buzzer, an unused cabinet in a corner. Nosy Corello will be sure to check the cabinet. Perhaps he'll reach inside, perhaps just press his face close and look. The shock of finding the snake, and maybe even being bitten by it, should overtax his heart. Should the device not cause a cardiac arrest, no suspicion falls on you. Trap failed. Traps often spring without catching anything. Should a grad student reach in there, the defanged snake cannot harm him or her. Again, no loss. You can perhaps try again sometime if another plan presents itself."

Dr. Osada sat motionless, expressionless, inscrutable. At length, he nodded slowly. "An error in your hypothesis. You said no suspicion would befall me—no way such a trap could be laid at my door. You just laid it at my door. Why?"

"Partial prints at the scene and the tires on your Toyota."

"Interesting. You anticipate taking me to jail?"

Joe shook his head. "You are not the only one to purchase that style of off-road tire. Many people do."

"What they call circumstantial evidence."

"Right. Very flimsy circumstantial evidence. Your defense lawyer would shred that bit of evidence instantly. Same with the partial prints. Not definitive enough to hold up in court. And even if they were, even if the tire tracks could be identified as yours alone, there is no reason you would not be among the many people who go out there sooner or later. Perhaps you're simply releasing some *Tantillas* there to see if they can survive in that environment. It's a good place for that; it's been analyzed so thoroughly, you know exactly what plants and animals are there. Controlled experiment. Or perhaps you're examining the area, checking the feasibility of doing further work. A dozen excuses. If I, an outsider, can find them, you surely could come up with some good ones."

"You're saying, therefore, that you've no certain way to prove it. Then why divulge your hypothesis to me?"

"To see your reaction to it."

"And my reaction tells you—"

"That my hypothesis is correct." By pulling his sleeve up as far as possible, Joe could just barely reveal the brown dots of scab, all that was left of his snakebite. He held it up for Osada to see. "You're lucky I have a strong ticker."

Dr. Osada's eyes widened; his face went flat. He smiled suddenly. "Not so lucky as you, my friend." The smile faded. "I admit nothing. Your hypothesis remains an untested, untestable hypothesis, but a clever one. Rattlers often get into those two little buildings. Students automatically check for their presence when they camp there."

"I regret being unable to prosecute. You're as guilty of attempted murder as is a person shooting with a gun. Fortunately, no harm was done."

His voice softened. "Corello was a blight on both science and humanity. He's the only person in the world about whom I've ever said that. I'm pleased that trap sprung harmlessly, if indeed it was a trap. Such an act would weigh heavily on its perpetrator, I'm sure. I know something about burdens. I carry many weights."

"Then I've another hypothesis. Your trap inflicted such a heavy psychological drain on you that you decided to act more precipitately. You killed him with Gila monster venom."

Again, Osada's features closed down shop. At length he smiled sadly. "No. No, that hypothesis is without basis."

"I've known murderers to lie, but I'll take your statement at face value for the moment. What other weights? Unburden yourself of them, if you would."

Osada looked at him with a frightened expression. The expression evaporated. "Personal matters. Very private. Nothing pertinent to your investigation."

"You'd be surprised what sometimes pertains. Try me."

Osada sat for long moments studying Joe's knees, and Joe was about ready to decide he'd get nothing further from the man. Osada's mouth opened and closed again. Silence. "I am happily married, detective."

Joe waited.

"About a year ago, I very nearly made the dreadful mistake of deliberately stepping outside the marriage bond. I did not, but the near miss, so to speak, rattled me. It still does. I thought I was superior to that sort of desire. I thought I would get over it. I thought I could expunge the guilt and remorse. So far I have not . . . not completely." His eyes rose to meet Joe's. "It's a foe I must wrestle to the ground by myself."

Joe waited. Nothing more came forth. Finally he nodded and sat forward. "Dr. Osada, you're still in the running as a chief suspect in this business. But the snake in the cabinet is too iffy to prosecute, unless we can come up with far more compelling evidence than my suppositions. One less weight in your backpack of burdens."

"Two less weights. I would not have thought that discussing my other problem, even circumspectly, would relieve me. I feel better, to quote the trite expression. Thank you."

Joe stood, so Osada stood. With pleasantries and a handshake, Joe left.

He was on a roll now. He'd guessed that one right. For the next phase of his multiple hypotheses, he would look up Jason Houser, and then John Lowry. He'd need backup for Houser. He walked down to the union, dug out a quarter, and stuck it in the pay phone to call Tommy.

Building

Joe watched Tommy pull his beetle into the fifteen-minute parking space and stroll up the slanting walk to the union in simmering, glimmering heat. As he came swinging in through the glass doors, Joe stepped forward. They met in the air-conditioned chill, the contrast between inside and outside made all the more extreme by the relentless late afternoon sun.

"Called his office." Tommy handed Joe a slip of paper from his pocket notebook. "Houser be at this address, a remodeling job in south Tempe just this side of Ahwatukee."

Joe pondered the address. He knew the block. It was one of those big storage warehouses being altered into an office complex. "Does he know we're coming?"

Tommy cleared his throat. "*We're* not. I've an appointment with his daughter. Yourself will talk with Mr. Houser. And aye, he knows you're coming. He'll not leave the site before ye arrive."

"Cancel your appointment. I need you for backup." Joe pushed out through the doors into the brilliant heat.

Tommy stared at him a moment. "A bit short, aren't ye?" He strode off down the angled sidewalk.

"Yeah. Now that you mention it, two or three inches shorter'n Houser, and I wouldn't put it past him to take a swing at me. I don't care to tug on Mr. Houser's whiskers all alone while you're having a good time playing around with his direct descendant. You can stick to business like you're supposed to be doing."

"No way to make contact with her to cancel."

"Leave word with Miss Watkins." Joe turned on his sulky partner. "We went through all this a couple months ago with Gretchen. Now it's Ruth. When you're in love you're a royal pain, and I don't intend to stick my neck in a wringer alone because you're off pursuing your current flame."

Tommy paused on the curb. "Nor does meself relish following a crabby partner about. Go home and take a cold shower and we'll both approach Mr. Houser tomorrow."

"We'll do it now. I want to clear this case while I'm still young."

Glaring, Tommy reversed and marched back inside, his elbows clearing a path three feet wide. Joe stepped off the walk to a nearby palm tree and leaned back against it. Its corklike scratchy surface irritated his skin and he didn't really care. Let Tom stew. This blowup had been building for a while. It would pass, with time. They always did.

And stew Tom did, before and after his brief call to the Life Sciences office, back out to his car, and all the way down to Jason Houser's construction site. Tommy pulled in beside a dozen dusty cars and pickups in a vast parking lot. The warehouse sprawled across the lot like an egg in a frying pan. The building must surely be a bugger to keep cool, for sunlight bounced off the tin roof, off the cinder-block walls, off the powder dust of the parking lot, out of the glaring sky. It broiled you from all angles.

A dozen steel garage doors studded the north wall. But only one of them had 100 tracks pouring in and out. Beside it, a zillion shoe prints went in and out a people-sized door. Joe and Tom entered by that one, from blistering heat into stuffy heat.

A few questions, a few wrong turns, and they found Houser, deep within a rat's maze of partitions and false walls. He had set up an office, or perhaps call it a command post, in an echoing room with no ceiling. Up in the dark rafters, the place was still a warehouse. Down here, an office was taking shape. A coffee maker gurgled in the corner. Stacks of blueprints spread themselves out and curled at the ends across several huge tables.

"Gentlemen." Houser smiled the first smile Joe had ever seen on the man.

Tommy was looking all around, barely short of gaping. "The air conditioning ducts, the pipes . . . meself has seen more orderly piles of spaghetti. How do ye manage to keep track of this?"

"That's what blueprints are for." Houser pointed.

"Up there's the old system. Not adequate for the new use."

"I see." Tommy nodded sagely. "Once all these partitions and rooms are in place, the old system cannot get into all the little cubbies, right?"

"Right. New sheet metal fabrication, new air conditioning system. It's one thing to serve a big open space, and something else altogether to serve these cubicles. Different air flow, different need pattern."

"Peak need? That sort of thing?"

"Exactly."

Joe saw a good opening. "Building like this—really knowing what you're doing—must be immensely satisfying. You mentioned once that you did work of this sort for your church. The same rules apply, I'd guess; different sorts of needs for the big sanctuary and the little nursery."

"Exactly." Houser headed over to the coffee corner. "Coffee? Might have some pop somewhere. I can ask."

"Coffee would be good." Joe walked over beside him. Houser poured and motioned toward the sugar. Joe dumped in a packet and tasted it. "Make it yourself?"

"No," and he said it as though the idea were unthinkable. "Carla makes it when she brings the mail and messages out."

Tommy had been staring off into space. He turned. "Mr. Houser, if your family needs a new car, who purchases it?"

"I do." Houser frowned. "Why?"

"Motor vehicle records indicate your wife drives a little Buick. She chose that herself, I trust."

"Chose it? What do you mean? She needed a car, and *Consumer Reports* rated that model best in its class. And I did some duct work for the Buick dealership in Gilbert. He gave me an excellent deal."

"So she didn't buy it."

"I bought it for her. She doesn't work." He frowned. "I don't understand what you're getting at. Martha is a housewife, detective. None of this women's liberation stuff in our house. I support her, and I support her well; that Buick isn't any piece of junk."

"Did ye consult her at all in its purchase? How about the color? Did she pick out the color?"

Houser bristled. "What is this?!"

Joe purred, "Ephesians 5, right?"

"Exactly!" Houser glared at Tommy. "What are you getting at?"

Tommy shook his head. "Satisfying a surmise meself made previously."

Joe picked it up. "We're here in regard to the death of Vic Corello, of course, but I have a personal reason for talking to you. Last April I committed my life to Jesus Christ. Since—"

"That's wonderful!"

Joe smiled. "So I'm finding out. Now I'm trying to settle into a church that will help me grow. You're so enthusiastically devoted to yours, I was hoping you'd tell me a little about your denomination. What you believe, that kind of thing."

"Let me first off invite you to service this Sunday. You can see for yourself. Summer hours are 8:30 in the morning and 6 in the evening, prayer meetings Wednesdays at 7:30, men's breakfast Thursday mornings at 6, meet at the church. We preach the pure Gospel, no liberal heresy."

"Thank you." Joe glanced at Tom. This was Joe's part of the conversation. He and Tommy had reviewed thoroughly where they planned to go. He just hoped Tom's mind wasn't wandering. "One point a friend has been arguing with me lately is this eternal salvation business. Not too helpful, really. He's got me more confused than anything."

"Easy to get confused on, there's so many opinions out there." Houser settled his backside down against a table edge, creasing the corner of a blueprint, and didn't seem to care. He was tackling a subject he obviously loved.

For ten minutes he recited Scripture from memory, building a case for eternal security. Once God has you in His hand, you can err grievously and you're still forgivable. He will punish you but not abandon you to hell. Tommy's eyes glassed over.

Joe summed it up before Tom fell asleep completely. "So 'once saved always saved' is completely, scripturally valid?"

"Don't let some people scare you. They claim God will throw you away. He says He'll never forsake you. You can trust His word over theirs."

"Even if you sin grievously?"

"There is only one unforgivable sin, and the person who has given his life to Christ cannot commit it." Houser laid a hand on Joe's shoulder. "You're safe. God forgives."

This was Tommy's prearranged cue, the conclusion of this discussion. He picked it up. "Whilst we're discussing sin, yourself be committed to a pro-life stance, aye?"

"Abortion is first-degree murder. Premeditated murder."

"Then you're aware, I'm sure, that your daughter has committed premeditated murder."

Houser changed instantly, from an enthusiastic preacher to a large and very dangerous belligerent. He pointed a trembling finger at Tom. "I warned Ruth about you, you foreign papist."

"Eh, she mentioned ye forbade her to come near me."

"Mr. Houser!" Joe stepped in closer to the man, ready to make a grab if he turned violent. "Even if your daughter did something like that, it's surely not a reflection on you. I mean, she's a grown-up, on her own. She's not a little girl under your roof anymore."

"The father is responsible for his daughter until she marries, whether she's fifteen or forty. You'll learn that as you study Scripture. I want this man out of my sight. Now."

Joe cranked up the tone of apology to full force. "I'm sorry. We're required to handle this investigation, Mr. Houser. I'm very sorry, but we have to explore this thoroughly."

"Don't give me that! You don't have to destroy reputations."

Tommy had moved back into a corner, partially behind a table, making himself as unobtrusive as possible. It was Joe's ball now.

Joe modulated his voice to a low croon. "I have a seven-year-old daughter. She's a handful now. In ten years . . . how in heaven can a man keep that kind of control over her in today's environment? It seems impossible to me. How do you handle it?"

It worked. The need to pontificate outweighed the fury. His voice softened as he launched into a lengthy and morose tale of how today's girls did what they wanted, resisting male supervision. He never called them women. Not once did he refer to Jesus Christ in any context whatever.

As he tried to keep track of all this, Joe found himself analyzing his own feelings for the man, and what he found was sympathy. He pictured himself in those shoes, trying to control what he could not control. Frustrating. The world was not marching to this man's drumbeat. Frustrating. Was the man frustrated enough to commit murder? The jury was out on that one. The guy certainly meant well.

Joe stepped into a break in Jason Houser's preaching. "I understand Vic's views and yours were very similar. Is that correct?"

"In most things."

"Political matters. Moral and ethical matters?"

"For the most part."

"Are you familiar with the Svengali legend?"

Houser scowled. "What's that?"

"A powerful man exerts immense influence over an impressionable girl, shaping her and dominating her. *My Fair Lady* and other theatrical works are based on it."

Houser's scowl deepened.

"Could Vic Corello have exercised a Svengali-like influence over Ruth? Bending her to his will, using her? He was a powerful man in so many ways."

"What are you saying?"

"That he could have taken immoral advantage of her. She's young and beautiful and still not wise to the ways of the world. She needs protection, as you just pointed out so eloquently, but you can't protect her."

Houser shifted his glare to Tommy for no reason Joe could see.

Joe pressed on. "You said on another occasion that Vic would never defile a woman young enough to be his daughter. And yet, from what we've learned about Corello, it's not only possible but probable."

Houser wheeled on Joe so suddenly that Joe saw Tommy move, closing in on him. Houser dropped his voice to a menacing rumble. "If you so much as breathe a–" He stopped. Dripping hatred, he held Joe eye to malevolent eye. "My daughter's reputation is spotless. I know how you people work. This is all probably being recorded."

Joe shook his head. "It's neither legal nor admissible in court to–"

Houser blurted a highly uncharacteristic expletive. "I'm not going to say anything your lawyers could make sound like a threat. Let's just say if you speak one word that could damage my daughter's reputation–one single word–I won't take it kindly." Casually, in an exaggerated manner, he drew his finger across his throat.

"Understood, sir." Joe backed off. "Um, we're, uh, due in town for another appointment. I'd like to talk to you again in a couple days. Particularly, I'd like to hear more of your views on raising daughters." He whipped out his business card. "If you think of anything you believe we ought to know, here's our number."

Joe and Tom excused themselves, wished Houser a good day, what was left of it, and made their exit. It took a bit of doing to find their way back out through the maze. The building had been designed for one thing; now it was being redesigned for something else. Buildings should remain what they were designed for.

Joe hit the big steel warehouse door and hauled it up and open. A blast of heat flung itself against him. Beautiful, natural heat, and the freedom of open sky.

"Why did ye curtail the interview so quickly?" Tommy headed for his bug. "All we got was religious mumbo jumbo. Nothing helpful."

"A lot helpful. Mrs. Houser isn't allowed to think for herself."

"Ye truly lend credence to that theory of unfinished business and such? The daughter playing out her mum's desires?"

"Could be significant." Joe slipped into the bug; his whole backside instantly soaked up the heat of the burning seat.

"Meself hates playing the heavy in these scams," Tommy jammed his key into the ignition. "That be Ruth's father I just alienated. And to what end?"

"We found out from his own lips what we wanted to know."

"Methinks you're overemphasizing what ye heard at that meeting. They be not professionals."

"Maybe."

They rode in silence back uptown. They flipped a

coin for dinner. Heads, fast burger; tails, fast chicken. Chicken won. It was Tommy's turn to buy tonight, but Joe didn't press it and ended up with the check.

Distraction is what cost him the price of dinner. It seemed as if he were working on three or four jigsaw puzzles simultaneously, drawing from one big common pile of pieces. Every time he saw something come together, something else seemed to say, "Oh, yeah? Then what about. . . ?"

Osada. Dorothy Stearns. Houser, a powerful and determined and tormented man.

And Ruth. A picture of Ruth was emerging too. It was not a picture he liked in the least. Not in the least.

In Cold Blood

It was 7 at night, or thereabout. Joe could hardly expect anyone to be left at VARI at this hour. Miss Watkins went home by 5, and probably so did everyone else, except maintenance.

"Maybe maintenance can tell us who goes in and out of that coffee room at odd hours," he suggested, and Tommy took the hint. They pulled by the U, parked in a half-empty lot close to the building—that had to be a first—and began exploring halls.

Tommy's snit seemed to have abated somewhat. He wasn't quite as ebullient as usual, but he had sweetened enough that Joe no longer felt like strangling him.

"Past 7 o'clock." Joe stopped.

Tom looked at him.

Joe grimaced. "That special deal on tickets to England. It expired exactly one hour and—" he looked at his watch—"fifteen minutes ago."

"Do not tell me ye regret it already."

"Okay, I won't tell you." *I've just robbed my kids of the opportunity of a lifetime. Who knows how much longer the grandparents will live? What if they die before the kids ever see them? And all because of a freckle-faced girl in Waukesha.* He dragged his mind away from the acute disappointment in himself and put it to the task at hand.

Nearly all the doors were locked. Joe expected that. The cage room was absolutely secure. They found no one around.

At the other end of the hall they passed an open lab door, the lights off inside. Tom hung a fast left and stepped inside it. He flicked one of half a dozen switches and the recessed overhead at his end of the room flared on.

"I could use a cold drink. Yourself?"

Joe preferred his room temp, but on a day like today, with the thermometer pushing 112 until evening, cold or no-cold didn't really matter. "Sure."

Tommy headed for a refrigerator in the corner. "They keep a supply in here. Meself shall replace it with a six-pack then." He swung the door open.

"You're getting to know your way around here. All the nooks and crannies."

"Only those crooks and nannies serving me stomach."

A dozen cotton duck bags stacked on the first and second shelves practically blotted out the fridge light. Behind the bags, a crowd of soft drink cans tried to peek over. Tommy made two tries at reaching a can without disturbing anything. Even his lanky fingers couldn't do it. He dragged one of the bags off the shelf and out. Then he pulled another one out.

Tommy yelped suddenly and dropped them both. Joe's gun was in his hands before the bags hit the floor. Talk about being on edge . . .

Tommy leaped backward a giant step. " 'Tis alive!" The smaller of the bags remained closed. From the loosened mouth of the larger one, a broad brown diamond head emerged. Like toothpaste from a tube, a thick, fat, patterned snake extruded itself slowly, pausing about halfway out of the bag. *Not again!* and *Now what!* echoed in Joe's rattled brain.

Joe licked his lips and took deep breaths. He could not quiet his jangling nerves. "There's gotta be a snake stick around somewhere close, or a broom handle." His voice cracked. This was embarrassing, not to mention frustrating. He was accustomed to snakes. They had never bothered him before . . . until that gray rattler, leaping out of the darkness at him . . .

Tom backed away, watching the gruesome thing as if it might leap at him. He ran to the door and hit all the light switches in the panel. The room blazed bright.

Joe watched the muzzle of his own gun bob around. He stood at best a 10 percent chance of hitting the thing, should he have to pull the trigger. During the majority percent, the gun muzzle was swaying wildly through some other part of its arc.

The door swung open. Help at last! Miss Watkins,

the perky little secretary, took two steps inside. "Oh, good. I thought I saw you two come in he—" She froze. Her hands flew up in front of her face and she screamed, the way women always scream in those 1950s horror flicks. Forget help. She contributed to the further destruction of Joe's nerves by screaming again.

In a fascinating parody of a slow-motion nature film, the snake squeezed itself forward out of the bag, until its stubby tail flicked free. Never had Joe seen such an obese version of your basic snake shape. Leaving the bag behind, it moved forward lethargically. It had trouble gaining a purchase on the slick cement floor. It squirmed more or less in place and then extended its head off into another direction.

Miss Watkins disappeared.

Joe listened to Tommy rummaging in cupboards and closets and drawers. Tom appeared at his side with a large piece of bedsheet. "Do ye suppose 'twill go to sleep if we cover it up?"

"Try."

Tom snapped the sheet out wide open above the snake. The stained whiteness fluttered down over all but the blunt little tail. The sheet settled. It moved. The tail tip withdrew from sight beneath it. About the time Joe drew a breath of relief, the sheet began to move again. The head poked out. Here it came, still in slow motion, struggling for traction.

John Lowry appeared in the open doorway. "Susy said . . . oh. It's only him."

Joe glanced at Lowry. The bushy brows tucked together in a sort of frown as Lowry stared at the snake, but it was not a worried or puzzled frown. More a thoughtful one.

"Don't shoot it," Lowry said. "I'll get a stick." He left. Eons passed. Two or three minutes later he returned with one of those snake sticks. With a casual flick of the stick, he flipped the bedsheet piece aside. With another, he scooped up the cotton duck bag.

"Here. Hold this." He thrust the bag toward Joe.

What could he do? Joe holstered his gun with deep, deep foreboding. He gripped the mouth of the bag and the whole thing vibrated uncontrollably. He couldn't stop trembling. It angered and embarrassed him all over again. Who would imagine that one little gray *Crotalus mitchelli* could do that to a person?

Firmly, deliberately, oh so smoothly, Lowry manipulated the stick to pick up the snake by its narrow little neck. It flopped about on the end of the stick, but not very enthusiastically. Lowry grabbed the mouth of the bag with his free hand and, with Joe's grip, pulled it open into a huge three-cornered hole.

He lowered the thirty inches of snake into the gaping bag. When the head disappeared below the rim he released it. A yank of the cord shut the bag.

Crisis past.

Joe stood numb, staring at Lowry. Lowry looked at the refrigerator still hanging open. "Who's taking pictures?"

"What?"

"Looks like someone is cooling the kids off for a photo shoot." He took the big cotton bag out of

Joe's hands, picked the other up off the floor, and let them dangle casually as he peered in the fridge. "Regular or diet?"

"Regular."

Lowry pulled two cans, tucked them under his arm, pulled two more and gently laid the sacks back on the shelf. He closed the refrigerator. Ah, sweet closure.

Joe walked over to the nearest stool and sat down heavily, leaning his weary body against a lab counter. "What was that, anyway?"

"Rhinoceros viper. African swamps."

"A whole refrigerator full of that stuff." Joe's nerves still weren't cooperating.

Tommy shuddered. "I don't mind saying this be absolutely the worst, most nerve-racking case meself has ever experienced. The blinking worst." He relieved Lowry of two pop cans and delivered one of them to Joe. He popped the lid on his. "What's this about a photo shoot?"

"To take clear pictures of photogenic herps instead of blurred pictures of fast-moving herps, you cool them off overnight. They get so sluggish you can take your time, even pose them any way you want. They just sit there."

Miss Watkins appeared in the door, looking pale.

"Who's doing the photo shoot?" Joe called to her.

Her attention shifted from the refrigerator to Joe. Ever so cautiously she stepped into the room. She crossed to Joe and the lab counter. "A man from a publishing company called Adventure Books is sending a photographer over tomorrow. Gary sent him a list of the animals we have and he checked off the ones he wants to take pictures of. The company pays the department a fee."

Tommy offered her a lab stool. She plopped on it. Lowry handed her a soda can. She looked at it, glanced at the fridge, and popped the can open. Obviously, she would have preferred diet. Just as obviously, she was not about to ask for a switch.

Minor little revelations stirred at the back of Joe's brain. "So Collier put all these bags of animals in the refrigerator. Is he the only one who puts things in the fridge? I mean, are there assigned tasks in the department and that's one of his?"

Miss Watkins shrugged.

Lowry took a swill. "Anyone who wants a cold snake can stick it in the fridge. If you see a bag in there already, you tag yours so they don't get mixed up."

"So if none of these bags has a tag, that means the same person put them all in there."

"Right."

"Is there a record kept? If you were to refrigerate a snake or lizard, would you write it down somewhere?"

"Nope. Nobody gives a healthy slug what you do with your snake. Take it home and put it in your own fridge if you want. If your wife'll let you."

"Do you leave a note in the snake's cage, or somewhere, so that if someone counts noses, he or she doesn't report it missing?"

"Collier probably wouldn't. He counts the noses. Besides, when a couple dozen critters are gone and their cage doors are standing open, you assume the fridge is full."

"Why not assume some eco-maniac turned them loose?"

"Good point."

Tommy twisted on his stool to address the secretary. "Miss Watkins, methought ye went home at 5:00."

"Four-thirty, usually, but I've been working late. We're processing department records on the incoming majors. You know, the biology majors entering this fall. Cynthia gave me some files to give you when you came around. From the chairman's office. They're upstairs."

"We'll stop by then." Joe smiled at her.

She smiled back. She hesitated on the stool a moment. "Guess I'll get back there, then." Pause. "Well, uh, um, good-night."

"Good-night, Miss Watkins."

She looked at Tom. "Shall I bring the files down here?"

Tom hauled himself up off his stool. "Meself shall escort ye up and get them now."

"Thank you." She led the way out.

Joe watched them go. Lowry started to stand up. Joe raised a hand. "A few minutes of your time, if I may."

He settled down again. "What can I do for you?"

"Couple things. One, did you ever approach Ruth or were you approached by her sexually?"

Lowry stiffened instantly. "Of course not! I'm married."

"You know and I know that's no guarantee. Dr. Lowry, I'm not looking for lurid details. A confusing scenario is plaguing my mind and I need your honest response on this."

"I don't see how it pertains."

"In a puzzle of 1,000 pieces, let's say you have 100. I have 900. Can you truthfully say you can tell how each of your 100 pieces pertains, without knowing what my 900 look like?"

He stared at Joe for a few moments. His eyes drifted away. He stared at nothing at all through the formica lab surface. "When I learned for certain she was sexually involved with Corello, I desperately wanted to lure her away from him. I couldn't stand the thought of him . . . he was a predator. Sex, control, finances, everything. A predator. And she's so innocent. She didn't have a chance. But I didn't. No. I never approached her or was approached by her."

"Thank you. Next item. The two snakes out in the compound. They were put there by two different people."

"Why do you say that?"

"Assuming that someone would not handle them unless that person felt comfortable working with deadly snakes, that person would also know that the cobra is a predator of other snakes. If the person wanted to put two in, he or she would put in something other than a cobra, which might cancel out the mamba before it bites the victim. You don't put a snake-eater in with another valuable snake if you have an ulterior purpose for them both. Therefore, someone slipped the mamba in, while someone else, not knowing about the mamba, put the cobra there."

Lowry's abundant eyebrows rose. "Any line on who did what?"

"Nothing definite. A multitude of surmises, though. The suspects would be persons with easy access to the hot room with the poisonous snakes. Probably not Dorothy Stearns or Philip Osada, for reasons I won't go into. Possibly, but I can't say probably, not someone who knew that Craig would go in there to police the grounds—that's assuming the trap was laid for Corello. They wouldn't want Craig taking the bite accidentally. Most of the staff knew about him and his job. Ruth did, for example. I don't think you did." And Joe skewered him with a steady gaze.

"What are you saying?"

"If I had to rank the candidates for putting a mamba in the compound, or a cobra, I'd place you at the top of the list."

"Why?"

"You knew about Corello's lizard project in there, but you do not concern yourself with the normal day-to-day of the department. For example, you had no idea who specifically employed Craig. You were intensely disturbed by Craig's death. Most of all," Joe paused for effect, "I'm watching your face and hands right now. They're betraying your thoughts. You're a lousy liar, Dr. Lowry. Or rather, you're lousy at concealing the truth."

Tom appeared in the doorway and stood there silently, listening, avoiding breaking the spell.

And Lowry crumbled, literally and figuratively. He melted forward, both elbows on the lab counter, and buried his face in his hands. Joe waited.

When eventually Lowry raised his head, his eyes were still dry, but his face looked stricken. "When I learned the mamba hit Jim Craig, I–" He shuddered. " 'Devastated' is putting it mildly. Craig was such a splendid . . . I was so certain only one person would ever go in there. Oh, sure, kids get in once in a while, but security kicks them out before any harm is done, and that doesn't happen often. Only Corello messed around the rock piles a lot."

"You deliberately released the mamba, then, to bite Corello. It was the mamba, right?"

Lowry nodded. "Put it in a bag and lowered it out a window. It was so easy. When I talk about it now, it sounds miserably cold-blooded."

"What drove you to it?"

He turned sad, sad eyes to Joe. "The son of a buck was damaging so many people, Rodriguez. So many. He was ruining me. I'd exhausted all my appeals. I'd be out of here next year and nowhere to go, and all because of him. Know why he hated my guts? I'm pro-choice and he's pro-life. I don't even believe in abortion without constraints. I mean, I don't think a person should be allowed an abortion any time; there should be some sound reason besides inconvenience. But that wasn't good enough. He did his best to destroy my career because he didn't totally agree with me on that one issue, and he wouldn't allow any latitude. None at all. Nothing about professional competence or scholarship."

"Why didn't you complain formally? Or did you?"

"Who'd believe me? It's so insane, so ridiculous-sounding. No one would believe the eminent Dr. Corello would be that despotic and narrow-minded. But the cobra. I honest to God don't know how the cobra got in there, or why."

Bugged

Joe knew the fellow standing beside Lowry only very casually. A criminal defense lawyer, the guy was pretty good at getting his clients reduced charges; rarely was he able to pull a client off the hook completely.

Jerry Hocks, Joe's lieutenant, knew him too. Jerry, his salt-and-pepper head bobbing, stood nose to nose with the legal wonder, arguing. Lowry sat oblivious, ten feet away on that lab stool, while his lawyer and the lieutenant blew smoke at each other.

Doug and Hack and Gretchen all swarmed over Lowry's office and this lab. Joe had no idea what they expected to find, and they probably didn't either. This case would likely end up manslaughter at best, rather than attempted murder, and it wouldn't be won with forensic evidence anyway.

Tommy moved in beside. "Ye called that one out of

the hat. What next?"

"I'm wondering about Gary Collier. I'd put him next on the list, I think."

"Confront him? Sneak up on him? Get him boozed up again?"

"How about you talk to him downtown? Get him off his turf and feeling uncomfortable."

Tommy nodded.

Joe added, "Except he's not home. I tried his apartment a couple times now. No answer. Nor at his office here, either."

"Do ye suppose he'd have a date or appointment written down on a desk calendar?"

"Let's go look."

Joe broke into the argument before him without compunction, said a few words to Jerry and headed upstairs with Tom. Normally, he would have taken the stairs by preference; he always preferred stairs to elevators for anything under six floors, even when the elevators ran smoothly without being pounded upon. Tonight he would have taken the elevator, because his ankle was objecting to the stair climb. Tom bounded up the stairs though, so Joe followed, clear up to the fourth floor.

Corello's office, the one with all the windows, was at this end of the hall, Collier's windowless cubicle at the other. Joe and Tom came out of the stairwell, turned the corner, and headed past Corello's office and on down the hall.

Joe grabbed Tom's elbow and pulled him to a halt, motioning silence with a finger to his lips. It took Tom a moment to catch on; he must have been daydreaming again. Hang, but Joe hated it when

Tommy fell in love!

Corello's office had been sealed ever since his death. It wasn't now. Someone had removed the yellow police tape. Quickly, silently, Joe moved in very close to Corello's office door and listened. Carefully he grasped the doorknob by two fingers, lest he mess up prints. He twisted. Unlocked, it quietly opened. A dim blue light filled the crack.

Tommy pulled his weapon. Joe took a deep breath and balanced his own revolver in his hands. It was cool and heavy and it made him nervous. It always did. Tommy nodded. Joe nodded.

Joe slammed the door open, charged through the doorway and ducked aside against the wall, gun leveled. Instantly Tommy was in behind him.

Gary Collier yelped, terrified, then bolted halfway out of the chair at Corello's desk. The blue light from Corello's computer terminal made the whites of his wide eyes glow. His hands and arms shot straight up, as high as they could reach.

Tommy cruised all four rooms of the spacious office, checking closets and nooks, securing the place. Joe kept his gun leveled on Collier, more for psychological effect than anything.

"No others," Tommy announced. He frisked Collier a bit more roughly than he normally did, and shoved the kid down into Corello's chair.

Joe picked up the phone and punched in Doug's cellular number.

Doug answered immediately, but that was to be expected; he kept his cellular in a belt holster.

"I'm upstairs in Corello's office. It's been compromised. Will you send someone up to go through it again?"

"Rats . . . Yeah. Ten minutes."

"Might as well send Jerry and some uniforms up too. We have an intruder here."

"Need help?"

"Situation's in hand." Joe holstered his gun.

Doug mumbled something—by habit he never said clear good-byes over the phone—and hung it up.

Collier, his hands cuffed behind him, was hearing his rights in an Irish accent. He didn't look too interested in his rights, but he did look worried. His eyes flicked from Tom to Joe to Tom and back. "Okay, so I broke a police tape. You caught me. But what I'm doing here isn't illegal."

"Your presence here be illegal enough." Tommy looked at Joe. "I suggest pulling Stan Newbury out of bed and hauling him down here to see what's happening. Stan can surely cast some light on our little drama."

"Good idea."

Tommy stepped into the other room and picked up the phone.

"Who?" Collier asked.

"We have a hotshot computer guru in the division who can talk to any machine anywhere anytime. Let him tell us what's going on here."

"I can do that. Tell you what's going on."

"I'd rather hear it from Stan."

"And I'd rather nobody but you know about it. Please. You don't realize how much is at stake here."

"Save it for when your lawyer's present."

"No! Please. Look. I'm not a criminal."

"Breaking and entering?"

"Well, yeah, okay. But not a *crime* type criminal. I mean, I'm not in here to commit a crime or anything."

"We'll let Stan tell us about that."

"Please!" Collier's voice took on a desperate, strident edge. "Listen to me!"

"Your lawyer—"

"Forget the lawyer! Just listen. I had this plan. It was a stupid plan, but it was a plan. I was going to ruin Vic. Ruin him professionally."

"Stupid, I agree. He seems to have been unassailable."

"I was doing some basic research for him. I have all the figures on my computer, and they feed into the mainframe. But his personal computer here, it's not tied into anything. He didn't trust anyone else being able to tap into his files."

"They can be locked up."

"He wasn't real comfortable around computers. He didn't trust passwords and locks. So I put a bug in his machine."

"A virus?"

"Right. He hadn't started work on that project yet—wanted to finish his video first—so he hadn't really looked at my results yet. After a given date—two days from now—all Vic's figures would be altered a little. It's a real beauty of a program, if I do say so myself. His figures wouldn't be the same as mine anymore. The new figures, the ones in his PC, would prove his case strongly; the actual figures are inconclusive."

Joe frowned. "In other words, the world would see Corello fudging his results to agree with some preconceived conclusion."

"That's it! And the mainframe and I, we'd have the original figures. After he published his results, using the data he thought I gave him, I'd confess he talked about sweetening the picture. I'd say he threatened me to keep silent, and I was scared and I did. But then I decided I had to risk everything and come forward because I value scientific honesty too highly."

"Which would fit the temperaments and personalities of you both, plus, make you a hero and him the villain. No one would ever trust his scientific work again." Joe nodded. "And it would have gone smoothly, except that suddenly Corello is dead. So he could no longer ostensibly alter the results two days from now."

"That's it."

Joe shook his head. "How could anyone connect the bug to you? So the virus did its thing—it couldn't be traced back to you. Why are you here now?"

"They'd figure out it was me. I'm the only one in the department who could do it. Ruth would have access to the computer, but she couldn't do it. She's not good enough. Not even Osada. Just me."

Collier sat back against his manacled hands. "I was simply going to let it slide. But then your department made hard copies of everything in Vic's machine—every program, all his data. And Phil ran off a copy of my stuff, and some other people's, for that meeting when we compared notes and tried to figure out what in blazes was going on with these research projects."

"So now everyone not only knows that your data is in Corello's machine—you couldn't simply erase it tonight; but also, everyone has that data, the true figures, the ones in the main memory."

"That's it. I had to come in here and kill the bug. Too many people have seen the original data now. If all of a sudden the data changed, they would figure out what happened pretty quick. The career that gets ruined would be mine. It still will be, unless you cut me a little slack. I'll take the rap for breaking in, no problem. But pulling the virus—that I gotta do. Please."

Joe glanced at Tommy standing in the doorway. "Sorry."

"Look, I don't have much to give you. I'm a grad student, for Pete's sake. But name a price and I'll do my best to meet it. Please."

"Bribery is also illegal."

He tipped his face ceilingward. His voice rose. "This is serious, Rodriguez! This is my professional reputation."

Joe kept his voice low. "Mine too. No bribe. No slack."

Doug came in with his video camcorder running. Hack followed behind with the toolbox. Since Joe was on the tape now anyway, he identified himself and Collier, briefly described what happened and walked out of frame.

Tom wagged his head. "Meself has never seen the likes of it. All these devious plots. The murderer need only have bided a wee bit of time and the whole thing would have been lifted out of his hands."

Gretchen came around the corner and paused in the office doorway. She looked at Joe. "I'll treat you to coffee—real coffee, no arsenic—at the twenty-four hour spot on Seventh." She looked at Tom. "I guess we're stuck with you too. I'll put up with it if you will."

Jerry, replete with uniformed reinforcements, arrived within five minutes. Joe turned the whole scene over to them and accepted Gretchen's invitation. When they left the floor, Collier was protesting loudly about not needing a lawyer, thank you, and was begging Jerry to listen.

Joe rode with Gretchen in her Toyota and let Tommy drive his bug over to the coffee shop in lordly solitude.

She cranked her air conditioning up and gunned the engine to make a light in time. "Mel Carter says I'm to tell you to take a running jump."

"His exact words?"

"No, I'm sparing you. He wasn't that nice. He liked the looks of Ruth Houser and tried to come on to her—to date her, at least. She's not interested. He used the word 'frozen' and a few other choice epithets."

"He's always had a gift for words."

"I think it really irritates him. He's not used to getting turned down, you know. "Mr. Handsome." I'm tickled pink! A girl with brains and guts."

"And he's blaming me because his line didn't work?"

"Or his many charms. He has this idea that you

guaranteed him a girl out of the deal."

Joe snorted. Down inside himself, he snarled, *Rats! Foiled again. If Ruth isn't interested in Mel, an exceedingly attractive man who knows how to move, she must be more than a little interested in Tommy. Double rats.*

At the coffee shop they found a booth in a rounded corner. Joe settled into the booth, the man in the middle. On one side Tommy sulked, either thoughtful or half asleep. On the other, Gretchen described the miserable absence of material they found to implicate Lowry in anything.

Gretchen jabbed Joe suddenly. "You're not listening."

"You're not saying anything. All I'm hearing are negatives."

"Okay, so you are listening. But your brain's going a mile a minute, and not on what your ears are telling it. What have you figured out?"

"Jonesy's death was not accidental, for one thing."

"Jonesy. That kid a couple years ago?"

"Fer-de-lance. Yeah."

"Ah!" Tommy sat forward. " 'Twas our hunch all along. What clinches it?"

"The details you told me about from the medical examiner's report—the coroner's report. Jones was alone in the venomous animals room cleaning cages. Following some sort of unspecified accident involving a fer-de-lance, Jones hit his head falling. The snake bit him and was still right beside him when he was discovered—a smoking gun, if you will."

"Aye."

"The report says he was discovered nearly three hours following death. Three hours. And yet that snake was still right there. It hadn't moved. The only good explanation for the snake remaining in one spot three hours is that it was refrigerated, and refrigeration spells premeditation. Ergo, Jones was murdered."

Tommy purred an expletive. "A precedent for what happened to Corello."

"Almost certainly the same murderer. Jones' death was ruled accidental. It worked once, so we use it again."

Gretchen chimed in. "And some twisted pervert who copycats murder wouldn't copy that one because, until just now, it wasn't considered a deliberate killing. So it's one killer rather than several."

Tommy nodded sagely. "Which still leaves the nagging question, 'Who?' "

Gretchen laughed grimly. "Easy. Corello committed suicide."

Joe looked at her. "Suicide!"

"No one else could have done it. John Lowry had a different trap laid. He's desperate, right? He's facing ruin. But he's too disorganized to set two at once. Not the good Dr. Osada, though he's desperate too. Too careful. And again, why set two traps?"

"Can't discount them," Joe reminded her. "They've both just demonstrated themselves capable of premeditated murder."

"That's true."

"Houser?" Tom asked.

Gretchen shook her head. "Much as I'd love to

pin it on him, he didn't have an opportunity. The cage room is kept locked. He couldn't gain access to the cage room, or the venom supply. Also, he probably wouldn't know which animal to release to match the venom used, since the venoms are labeled by scientific name—genus and species—and most of the caged animals aren't labeled at all."

Joe grunted. "Excellent point. Though he knows more about the operation than he lets on, I think. He seems to take pride in appearing ignorant."

Tommy picked up the train of thought. "Not Ruth, and undo everything she's been working on for years."

"Same with Gary Collier," Gretchen continued. "Besides, he's the wrong personality profile—liberal bleeding heart who wouldn't cause a physical death. Ruin the man's career, okay, but not murder. And he certainly wouldn't kill Corello with that virus thing hanging fire."

Joe nodded. "And place his own rep in jeopardy."

"And poor Dorothy Stearns had her own little plot brewing. That's a pun. No need for her to mess around with snakes." Gretchen lifted her hands helplessly. "You see? That leaves Corello himself. Clear as mud."

"The secretary, Sue Watkins."

Gretch snorted derisively. "That little fluffball couldn't find a grand piano in a one room house."

"Jealousy," Joe smirked.

Gretchen made a highly realistic gagging noise, but then, she'd been practicing lately. She turned pensive, and Tommy's face went blank as his thoughts drifted off elsewhere; so Joe sat silent, sipping his coffee, going over what he knew, over and over, and seeing nothing fresh or remarkable.

Gretchen spoke suddenly. "Impurity always comes back on you. You see? There's no escape from the consequences of impurity. God knows what He's talking about." She lapsed into silence again. Joe watched her a moment, puzzled. *What brought that on?*

And as his mind drifted away from the problem at hand, another tantalizing little bit of answer came. "He does too have access!"

"Who has access? You mean God? To what?" Gretchen and Tom both frowned at him, the only thing they'd agreed on in weeks.

"Jason Houser. He has access to the cage room, the labs, everything. I'll bet he does!" He looked at Tom. "That hunk of keys Ruth carries around. She has a key to everything, right?"

"Just about, aye."

"You told me she lost them at her home for a week. Her father could have stolen them, had them all duplicated, and given them back the next Friday when she returned. It would be easy for anyone to do, but especially easy for him. He installs locks and such. He deals with locksmiths constantly."

Gretchen's lovely eyes went wide. "In fact, he mentioned doing some ductwork for the U. It's barely possible he wangled at least some keys himself."

"If he thought Corello sullied Ruth's honor, aye, he might commit mayhem. But why the other deaths? Jones and Craig?" Tommy shook his head. "Never mind Craig. That was an accident, intended for Corello. But Jones?"

Gretchen sighed. "It's late. Too late. I'm drained. If I pay the bill, can we go home now?"

"You offered anyway, whether you can go home or not." Joe pulled his wallet. "I'll get the tip." He laid the money beside his coffee cup.

Gretchen paid, Tommy disappeared, and Joe stood around with his head churning. It was falling together, at least a little. Tom came back from the direction of the telephones and Joe followed him out to the parking lot. They waved good-bye to Gretchen as she drove away.

"You're pensive." Tom unlocked his side of the beetle. "Making sense of this rat's nest, I hope?"

"Mixed emotions. You're my partner and we depend on each other. But I'm not sure I like associating with a rapist."

Tom stopped dead and stared agape.

"Ruth." Joe leaned on the roof. As much as he hated this he forced himself to look Tom squarely in the eye. "She leads you on, initiates intimacy, paws all over you. Then at the last minute, she turns it around and doesn't want you near her. Particularly she doesn't want intimacy, even though she prepared for it. Fights you. But I get the message that you're fully intimate with her. You know and I know that if one of the partners resists, physically or verbally, that's rape."

For the first time since Joe knew him, Tom stood stunned, utterly speechless. He took a deep breath. "You've a splendid spy system going, somewhere."

"Tommy, for your own sake, break it off. A rape charge, even years in the future, will destroy your career."

For a full minute Tom glared at him with fire in those cool gray-green eyes, and Joe could not read what he was thinking. "Find your own ride home." Tom yanked his door open and slid inside. The motor roared. The beetle lurched forward and howled out to streetside. It barged into traffic as a pickup truck beeped its horn behind. The little green bug disappeared, swallowed in the dark of night.

Hungry

Ruth stared at her monitor, but she wasn't really seeing the figures. It wouldn't matter if she did. With Vic gone this project was useless. Worse than useless. It was taking time out of her life, peeling away minute after minute, hour after hour. She should abandon it and cut her losses right now instead of trying to salvage something. There was nothing to salvage.

The classical radio station finally finished its weather and Dow Jones averages and the figures at which gold and silver closed in London. Maybe all those numbers being spouted in her ears were messing her up. The disc jockey, if classical radio people can be called such, announced one of Ralph Vaughan Williams' folksong suites.

She hit Sort and keyed in a new combination. Maybe if she divided it all out this way . . .

The music caught her ear. It was an Irish tune, lilting and full of exuberance for life. Tom. He made everything right. He always did. His goofy grin, his bright demeanor, his cheerful wit—and then she thought about his touch. Everything. Respighi's *Pines of Rome* followed Vaughan Williams. She picked up the telephone.

She called Tom's desk, got a cheery recording, and left a recorded message as requested. "I'm hungry," she told the cold, faceless tape. "Can you come by this noon? We could go to lunch at that Thai place. I'll be in the cage room finishing up some chores."

Nearly an hour later her phone rang. At last!

He spoke no greetings, no words of love. He said simply, "I'm stuck here at Records yet for five or ten at most. That's meself coming through your cage room door." He hung up.

Her heart did a little trill and she allowed herself a smile. She took her time backing out of the program. She lived in dread of the moment she carelessly pushed a wrong key and erased everything. *Or perhaps erasing everything is the answer to all the woes that everything causes. Erase the source of woe. Everything is not the source of woe. Is there an answer? How does one cope with everything all at once, except just get rid of it? That's the way. Erase.*

She took the backstairs down to the cage room, let herself in, and flicked on the light. She checked the floor around, making certain nothing lurked, and took a turn through the room. She paused by the scorpion cabinet. She or Gary ought to milk them pretty soon. The schedule was running behind.

And the Gila monsters. She stood beside the terrarium awhile, watching them. She chose a particularly lovely one, lifted the lid and moved her arm in above it. With a snatch she grabbed it around the neck and jerked it straight up. It flopped in her hand and grew quiet, its bulbous tail hanging.

Idly she ran her finger down the delicately beaded skin. Gorgeous. She thought about how fitting it was that Vic was working on Gila monsters when he died. He was so like this lizard. Physically attractive. Dangerous. Stubborn, blunt-nosed, sharp of tongue and claw. She dropped it back in and closed the lid.

She paused briefly beside the gaping, empty cobra cage. Too bad about Tom shooting that other cobra. Now the department had only this *Naja*, and they would probably lose it too. She continued past the Mexican green rattler. It lay curled stock still, one unblinking eye watching her every move.

Snakes . . . so much symbolism attached to them. Evil. Satan. All the attributes her father inveighed against were embodied in these sleek, graceful serpents. Again she thought about Tom. Tom was evil; he led her on and took from her what no man ought take. Tom was sleek and graceful too. Tom and the *Naja* . . . they were made for each other.

Someone was rapping on the cage room door.

Jerry wasn't in his office but its door stood open, so Joe left his supplementals on the desk. He walked back to his own desk, feeling every step his left foot took. He should have reported his ankle before now. It wasn't getting any better; now pain frequently extended up his calf. Considering how he jumped from that window, a spiral fracture wasn't out of the question. Maybe he could get an x-ray where Fel worked and just pay for it himself instead of wading through these department forms.

Gretchen came in the far end as Joe was sitting down. She perched on the corner of Tommy's desk, across from him. "Hi, handsome. Is Mel talking to you yet?"

"H'lo, gorgeous." Joe sat back grinning. "He had no choice. He had to ask me to take his latest case; got some sort of suspicious death out at the race-track. Spent one hour on the scene and the next three hours in the public restroom. He caught that gut-rot bug."

"Couldn't happen to a nicer gigolo." Gretchen beamed. "I've been in the restrooms at the track. Definitely not Mel's milieu. So why aren't you out there?"

"Handed it off to Chen, who was passing through the office here at exactly the wrong moment. He just cleared the Fraser thing, so he has a hole in his schedule."

"Learning experience. Chen knows everything about baseball. Nothing about horses."

"Not an inkling." Joe stretched out and adjusted his ankle. "What can I do for you?"

She flopped down in Tommy's chair and stared across at Joe. "I'm hungry, Joe. Sexually, I mean. This celibacy is for the birds. And yet, I'm certain I'm doing the right thing. The more I think about it, the more I read, the more I'm convinced this is right. And the more I think about it, the more I'm sure that the hunger is for Tommy. Not just sex. Tommy. Know what I mean?"

Joe nodded.

"Joe? Do you think Tommy would be willing to start over? Courtship, keep it casual? See what blossoms? Do you think he can be a friend the way you are, without . . . " Her voice trailed off. "When you befriended me when I got sick, I felt so loved. Know what I mean? You weren't affectionate as such. No expectations or requests or demands. Freely given. It was just . . . just . . . love in action. I so much want something like that with Tommy. He's as gentle as you are, and sweet. But he's all on the surface. And bed-oriented. I want something deeper and wider than what we had."

"You know him better in some regards than I do. You'll have to talk to him."

She grimaced. "Where is he, do you know?"

"Down in Records, but from there I don't know. What's his calendar say?"

She glanced at his desktop. "Nothing beyond 10:30."

"Try his voice-messaging." Joe stood up and leaned out to Tom's desk to punch it in for her.

She put the receiver to her ear. Her face hardened. Joe thought he saw tears in her eyes, but the illusion passed.

She slammed the receiver down. "He's going to lunch with Ruth." She stared at Joe. Suddenly she stood up. "And I'm not going to sit back and watch it all go by. I'm going to Tempe to the Thai restaurant and show him what confrontation's really like. Want to do lunch?"

Joe grinned and stood up and reached for his sport coat. "Atta girl, Gretch!"

Daylight from the hall seeped under the door, a thin white line in the darkness. The rubber threshold was either compressing or wearing away. It ought to be replaced. Ruth sat up on the cage room floor. The line of light disappeared, so therefore it wasn't a very big gap yet. Still, why give escaped scorpions an easy way out? She'd put in a work order this afternoon.

And it had happened again. It wasn't her fault Tommy had taken advantage of her again. Like all the other times, these things happened in spite of her best intentions. She thought about her father's fury, should he learn about Tommy.

She thought about Vic.

She walked over to the door and flicked on the lights and squinted a few moments as her eyes adjusted, then pointed to the cabinets by the ceiling, over the lab table. "Tom, you're so tall; can you reach that binocular microscope up there?" She slipped into her rubber gloves.

Erase it all. Everything. That's the only way. Start over. We'll show Daddy, won't we?

He walked over. "With a bit of help, aye." He pulled a stool out from under the desktop and stood on it. He could just get to it. Somewhat smugly, as if manliness were related to reach of arm, he brought it down and handed it to her. He leaned over to scoot the stool back under the desktop.

Now! She swung the heavy metal microscope hard, but not as hard as she would have swung it a month ago. She had hit Vic much too hard. It aroused suspicion. The blow caught Tom behind the ear and knocked him five feet before he hit the floor. She raised the scope to swing again, but she didn't have to. He lay completely relaxed and still as the color drained from his face.

Quickly she grabbed lengths of rubber tubing from a drawer. Rubber tubing leaves no marks. She tied his right wrist to one table leg and his left wrist to another, stretching his arms out firm and tight. His gun. She pulled his gun. When this was over, she'd put it back. But she didn't want it anywhere near him just now.

She ran out, locking the cage room door behind her, and hurried down the hall to the other lab. Interesting, how Tommy just sort of dropped into her lap this noon. She didn't plan it. She didn't plan any of this. It all just happened. She yanked open the refrigerator, grabbed the bag with the cold cobra in it, scooped the venom vial out of the freezer compartment and ran back out. This was going very smoothly. Only a few minutes yet . . .

Gretchen's fingers diddled on her steering wheel as she waited for the light to change. Joe smiled to himself. She was mad now. Storming angry. Joe couldn't talk sense into Tommy. Mel couldn't lure Ruth away. Maybe Gretchen's impassioned confrontation would show Tommy she cared enough to risk everything.

He thought about all the puzzles left in their case here. Group them this way. Group them that way. What meshed? What jarred? What crucial detail was he ignoring?

"Gretch? Ruth Houser was raised ultraconservative. She invited Tommy to lunch, right?"

Gretchen called Ruth an unseemly name.

"I thought conservative girls weren't that forward. Let the man do the asking."

"Welcome to the modern age."

"Still, it's not what I'd expect from her. Repeat her voice message exactly, can you?"

She recited in singsong what she'd heard as she turned left off Mill Avenue.

Joe mulled it in silence, and with a jolt, everything fell into line. "Stop the car!" Joe grabbed her arm.

Scowling at him, she pulled aside and double parked.

Joe held her eye. "When you and Tommy made love, was it possible to stop him?"

"What?" She scowled at him harder. "I'd prefer to keep a few things private, even from his partner."

"This is important, Gretch. From what you know of Tommy, can he be guilty of de facto rape?"

"Joe . . ."

"Speculate. Please."

"This isn't a simple case of voyeurism, is it?" She thought about it a couple moments and he gave her the time. "Yeah. He'd never force himself on a girl, or even push the matter. But once he got started, yeah. If she let him go just so far, he'd reach a point where it was no longer her choice. I guess that's rape." The scowl softened. "Joe, what's this all about?"

"Turn left right here."

"The Thai restaurant's—"

"Turn!"

She pulled into the left turn lane and leaned forward against the wheel to watch the light. "What's going on, Joe?"

"I've been sorting the puzzle. Two classes of people: men Jason Houser liked and men he didn't like. Two other classes: Ruth's sexual conquests—more precisely, men she may have known carnally, and the men who would not be seduced."

"Tommy is a conquest."

"I'll explain later how I got the pattern of grouping. The bottom line is, the men who were intimate with her died. Craig, Corello, Jones. The men who were not intimate with her for one reason or another—Lowry, Osada, Gary Collier—are still alive."

Her knuckles turned white on the wheel. "And the spider is luring in the fly as we speak. Down to the cage room. Why now? She wouldn't do him now. It's a tryst. That's all."

"Maybe."

She drove in silence a few moments. "Serial killers, Joe. The time between killings keeps getting shorter and shorter."

"Stop here, Gretch. We can't drive the car any closer to Life Sciences than we are right now." He jumped out and ran for Life Sciences the moment she screeched to a halt and double-parked. No such thing as running. His ankle slowed him to a painful, galloping stride-bonk, stride-bonk, stride-bonk through the noonday furnace of the campus grounds.

The gum trees and palms offered scant respite when the summer sun burned this intensely. Gretchen kept up easily in her three-inch spikes. They hit the big glass doors as Osada and two companions were coming out.

Joe stopped, slightly winded, and plunked himself squarely in front of the Japanese gentleman. "Doctor, this is very important. The incident you told me about, the burden. Was it Ruth Houser?"

He hesitated only the barest of moments. "Yes."

"Go back inside and call the cops. Instantly!" Joe shoved past him into chilling air conditioning.

Here was that other lab with all its lights on. As Joe hobbled past he noticed—and hauled to a stop, backing up a step to make sure. His heart quailed. The refrigerator door was hanging open!

"The cage room! Run! She has a cold snake!" Joe yanked his gun as he bolted forward.

Gretch kicked her shoes off in two strides as she ran. By the time she was halfway down the hall she was sprinting with her gun in hand. She cast her purse aside.

Joe struggled to halfway keep up. Stride-bonk! Stride-bonk! Stride-bonk! They'd be too late. He took too long to figure it out. She had the snake ready when she called him this morning. She was way ahead of him. Too far ahead of him. All he could think of was Jim Craig as snake venom drained the life out of him.

Gretch lunged against the cage room door. She rattled the knob. As Joe approached she pressed her gun against the doorknob and her body against the wall. She turned her face away as she blew the doorknob apart, her .38's thunderous boom bouncing up and down the hall.

Joe hit the door full weight with his shoulder; it gave at the shattered lock and sucked him into the room. He saw Tommy on the floor. He saw Ruth kneeling over him with both hands close by his throat. He heard Gretchen's gun beside him roar again. Again. Ruth slammed back against the table. Her upper body exploded in blood and shrieks.

The hypodermic syringe she was holding sprayed a thin, arching stream into the air before it dropped from her hand.

* * * * *

"Joe?" To his right in the padded corner booth, Gretchen stared at her steak absently. "Okay. The men Ruth seduced died and the men she couldn't lived. But how did you finger her?"

"Aye." Tommy at Joe's left paused momentarily in his attack on the Chico's Rincon special combination plate. "Ye figured it all out. What tipped ye off?"

Joe laid his fork down. "As you said. Also, look at the similarities between Jason Houser and Vic Corello, particularly as Ruth would see them. Both of them, in essence, insisted her future depended upon their largess, Vic for her career life and her father for her personal life. He enforced on her that her eternal future depended on toeing his mark, following his beliefs without deviation."

"Aye, but she didn't toe his mark." Tom frowned. "She was well practiced sexually when meself fell into her trap."

"You didn't fall, you jumped." Gretchen glared at him.

Joe raised a hand. "Children; you're observing a truce, remember? Tom's point is good. She rebelled in several ways—her manner of dress, her promiscuity, even her study of snakes. The abortion was perhaps the ultimate rebellion, because both men were so adamantly opposed to it. I wonder if she did it with or without Corello's knowledge. We'll never know for certain."

Gretchen nodded. "She transfers the fear and rage she feels toward her father onto Corello."

"And others. She showed no interest in Lowry or Mel Carter. Those men were okay in Daddy's book, or were at least perceived so. Clean white bread, both of them. Men Daddy approved of didn't get seduced. That would not serve the rebellion. I'm fairly certain she and Craig were an item, though. Craig was black. She made an attempt on Osada, probably much the same way she initiated the relationship with Tommy."

"A black and a Japanese. I see! Miscegenation. The ultimate fear of every bigoted father." Gretchen was confirming what Joe had been thinking, and her educated confirmation felt good; she had a degree in psychology as well as forensics.

"And meself be Catholic and foreign born." Tom sipped at his iced tea.

Gretchen sat forward. "Wasn't Jonesy perfect for her? At least that's what Dorothy Stearns thought."

"Who knows?" Joe shrugged. "Jason Houser has so many narrow opinions, Jonesy could be on his blacklist for some reason we don't know. Because Corello was on Jason Houser's good side, he likely did not appeal to her sexually. Probably he, not she, initiated their affair, as a condition of her career advancement."

"Or . . . " Gretchen inserted, "she came onto him because of the rage transfer aspect. Lure the surrogate father figure into heinous sin. Doesn't matter. The end would be the same."

"Right. Houser almost certainly has some notion of what was going on. He quite probably warned her away from Corello, just as he warned her away from Tommy."

Tommy stared at his sweaty tea glass. "She approaches Osada sexually; he succumbs to her wiles, which be considerable; at the last moment she fights him off. Remorseful, he becomes her protector, trying to make up for a situation he thought himself had nearly caused." Tommy looked at Joe. "I aver it never clicked in his head that sweet Ruth was the aggressor; neither did meself."

Gretchen's voice dripped disgust. "That's because your typical male is so hung up on himself, he thinks it's logical when a girl melts into his arms. The illusion of being irresistible—it's on the Y chromosome."

Joe smiled. "One thing we failed to realize was that Ruth was past reason—past recognizing or caring what Corello's death would do to her career. She was no longer rational."

Gretchen shook her head. "Then Ruth put the cobra out there, right?"

"Yes, to get rid of Jim Craig. As a black, he was

on Daddy's 'no' list; therefore she seduced him. No doubt he participated eagerly in the seduction; therefore she marked him for death. Unlike Lowry, she had several ways of knowing he'd go out there cleaning up, and when."

"So Craig was the intended victim after all." Tommy waved a finger. "You'll remember how shocked she was, and yet not that a snake had done him, but that a thin black snake had done him. She was expecting a cobra; we described a mamba."

"Why kill her lovers?" Gretchen asked. "Never mind. I see. To negate the rage she was transferring. Society doesn't let her think about killing Daddy, so she transferred the hatred to substitutes and killed the substitutes. I'd guess too, Joe, that it was also to blot out the sin somehow. She rejected her own sexuality—"

"Split it off." Joe was learning the lingo.

"Right. But you can't do that. Human beings are sexual creatures, with hormones working all the time. So she—"

"Me point precisely in all this." Tommy interrupted. "Ye cannot split off what's a natural part of ye. Ye cannot turn it on one day and off the next, like a water faucet."

"Denying and abstaining are two different things." She twisted to face him squarely, for the first time that evening. "I am not denying my sexuality. I'm choosing not to exercise the physical aspect of it. That's a big, big difference. Acknowledging and dealing with it is the opposite of splitting it off." She sat back. "So she commits sin, or lets it be committed on her person—satisfying her sexual needs—

and then acts irrationally to erase it. Kill the sinner, expunge the sin. Or, kill the person blamed for the sin, expunge the sin. The head does some nasty things way down inside."

"Religion!" Tommy snorted derisively. "Now ye see, Gretchen, why your sudden obsession with religion puts me off so."

And suddenly a light dawned. "No, Tommy." Joc leaned forward. "Gretchen's interest is in serving Jesus. Pleasing God out of love. That wasn't Ruth's case."

Tommy grimaced. "Aye, now that I recall, when I asked her of her faith, she said 'nothing.' It did not signify at the time. 'Twas me error in discounting it."

"Jason Houser put on the trappings and made the show. That's not faith. It's not even really religion. And remember when we talked to Houser in the warehouse? He never once mentioned Jesus Christ."

"I did not notice."

"Houser not once said anything about serving the Lord. It was all mental exercise and external behavior. All sterile legalism. And that's the whole difference. Gretchen's 'crisis of conscience' as she calls it comes from wanting to please God. It has nothing to do with appearances. She's acting from the heart. That's real faith."

Gretchen pushed her plate away suddenly. "I'm sorry. This food is all very good, but I can't eat. Guess I'm just not hungry."

"You'll feel better, lass, with time. You've been through the wringer these last few days." Tommy leaned forward enough to take her hand in his. "I cannot tell ye how deeply I feel this. There I was on the floor and utterly helpless, still addled, vaguely knowing what was about to happen, and unable to speak, less move. She had the needle in me neck; I felt it prick. Then yourself comes blazing in and stopped her short of pushing the plunger all the way. Ye know how I spent those two days in hospital, just getting over the bit she got into me. 'Twas a gift of love I cannot—"

"No, Tommy!" Gretchen exploded. "It wasn't a gift of love. It wasn't a personal thing for you or her or me or anyone else. If it had been someone besides you on the floor, if you were a person I hated most and Ruth was a person I loved, I still would have had to do it. Hang it, Tommy, she was in the act of committing murder!" She stood up. "Excuse me, gentlemen, I'll be back." And she headed for the restroom.

Joe picked up his fork. "She's right, you know. Making it impersonal is the only way she can live with it. She's an officer, Tommy, doing an officer's job."

Tommy sighed. "I suppose so."

If Gretchen had not stopped Ruth in the act, how could they have ever proven her guilt in court? Joe pondered the question and decided it had no answer. But then, it didn't need one.

He heard an English accent as two people passed by, and remorse stung him anew.

Tommy shoved his empty plate aside. "What be ye contemplating now?"

"Aah, nothing. Feeling bad about letting that England deal slide by. Now that it's too late to take advantage of it, I regret not doing it, and it's weighing on me. I can go see Marie anytime. Late night flight, 1,000 miles max. I cheated the kids out of what might be their only chance to meet their grandparents."

"Really kicking yourself, aye? And well ye ought. Such good prices will not likely happen again."

"Thanks for the sympathy."

With a wicked, cunning grin, Tommy pulled a sheaf of envelopes out of his breast pocket and handed them to Joe. "I had me travel agent write ye up when she did mine. Yourself and the two kids. Ye owe me airfare."

"But they're nonrefundable. What if I—"

"I was not worried. Ye forget how well I know ye. And I already called Marie. I told her I took it upon meself to send ye to England, for ye were about to miss this opportunity for fear of disappointing her. Be there any heat, I'll take it. But I think there'll be none."

Joe opened his mouth. He closed it again. What could he say? He looked at them. London Heathrow, Heathrow to Shannon, Shannon to home. Just like he and Tommy had discussed. "I owe you infinitely more than airfare, my friend."

Gretchen returned, ready to sit down again.

Joe stood up.

Tommy pushed his chair back and rose. " 'Tis poor manners to leave the lad here before he's done. But Jose, if ye did not talk so much, you'd be finished by now. Gretch, may I take ye for a quiet chat and possibly a drink, just the two of us?"

She looked at Joe.

Joe sat down. "You kids go on. I'll take my time here. I have to fill out these stupid medical forms anyway."

She looked at Tommy.

"No strings attached." He pushed his chair in.

"No strings." She nodded slowly. "I'd like that."

Joe watched them leave. He tucked the tickets safely away in his inside pocket. He picked up his fork again and, with a sigh, dug out his medical claim forms, in triplicate. He was only on question 7. Last tetanus shot. *Who cares? Tetanus has nothing to do with a sprained ankle. Was it five years ago?* No matter. He wrote down "5 yrs."

Where would Tom and Gretchen go? Up to Los Olivos, probably. It was quiet there, and they both liked the place. In fact, that's where they went on their first date. Definitely Los Olivos.

And where was Joe going?

England.